Smoky Mountain Roots

ALSO BY RAY D. FORTNER, SR.

"BACKROADS OF THE MIND"
ISBN 0-9726365-0-1
Library of Congress Control Number 2005926227
Copyright 2002

"THE SHINY BADGE"
ISBN 0-9726465-1-X
Library of Congress Control Number 2005926228
Copyright 2005

Visit us at http://fortnerpublishingco.blogspot.com

Copyright © 2006 Ray D. Fortner, Sr.
All rights reserved.
ISBN: 0-9726365-2-8
Library of Congress Control Number : 2006900683

To order additional copies, please contact us.
BookSurge, LLC
www.booksurge.com
1-866-308-6235
orders@booksurge.com

RAY D. FORTNER, SR.

SMOKY MOUNTAIN ROOTS

A Novella Of The Trials Of A Young
Mountaineer Confederate Soldier As He
Matures And Settles In The South

2006

Smoky Mountain Roots

In remembrance of my Mother and Father, Levi Parker Fortner, and Mae Irene Baxter Fortner.

My everlasting gratitude to my wife Georgia Ann Fortner (Betty). She inspires, critiques, types, edits and assists with mapping and charting of the surfaces and reliefs ,of the region, which are in my books. She is a Corina (the heroine in the Novella called Betty) Her interests in my efforts has been unflagging.

Thanks to my great friend, Seldon Pierce, author, writer, journalist, and teacher. He is a learned gentleman who knows about writing and edits my work. He freely shares his knowledge of writing and life and his editing of my books still manages to build my confidence.

Throughout my writing career Mr. Pierce has been a mentor and advisor to me, akin to '"Sans Mantar, the loyal friend and advisor to Odysseus."

Maria Wilson who owns four Mustang horses shared information which enabled us to know Cody, the horse that Buck rides, and is based on her real Mustang, Cody. She has been most kind. Her knowledge and love for the wild Mustang is monumental. She is a supervisor with the

Florida State Forestry Department.

Mrs. Janice Warmack, Master of Science, Education, retired from the Escambia County, Florida school system as a career Counselor. She did a masterful job of editing this manuscript and The Shiny Badge.

Mr. Richard Slack, Captain Civil War Reenactment for his technical advice on Civil War. He furnished era clothing for the soldier on the cover.

Dr. Donald P. Hines, PH D, Police Psychologist. Retired from Guam Police Department. He read Smoky Mountain Roots and wrote the Introduction. His advice continues to be invaluable.

Story Ray Fortner, photo of young Civil War soldier. Grandson and namesake. Thank you Story.

Spud Heinzerling, Jet pilot and friend who was the jet pilot in "The Shiny Badge", owns Orso the Alaskan Malamute featured in Smoky Mountain Roots.

Mathew Linnville, professional photographer, cover pictures.

INTRODUCTION

This is the story of a boy becoming a man. A coming of age tale set within a backdrop of the most traumatic event in this country's history; The Civil War.

We follow the main character, Buck, as he makes every effort to stay alive in an environment which is doing its best to cut his young life short. As has been noted in all wars, time becomes accelerated and encapsulated at the same time. It is no different for Buck. Each event in this story has Buck growing into manhood at a far faster pace than would have been possible under less extreme circumstances. Deceptively it simultaneously creates an impression of time standing still.

There are few events that impress upon the psyche more dramatically than death. Buck is exposed to the reality of death in a manner which causes him to protect his sensibilities by living by a code of behavior which he feels is right for him regardless of the opinions of others.

The author paints a view of the beauty of the geography in which the story's events take place, which is in sharp contrast to the horror being experienced by the men, women and children who occupy this land.

As the tale unfolds it becomes obvious that circumstances have conspired to cause Buck to refocus his goals, while at the same time he hangs on to a few basic truths; such as his identification with his family, and his growing feeling for Corina, the girl he left behind. His values were forged into his very soul within the family, as well as the messages he accepted from the church. While keeping his faith in God, Buck lost his faith in the law to protect him and his young family.

Buck was blessed with physical attributes, as well as a serious demeanor, which men could identify with, and women saw as admirable. While possessing a limited education, there was an intelligence which Buck utilized to get himself out of a number of potentially dangerous situations; most notably his knowledge of how to succeed at hand-to-hand combat, while not feeling the need to humiliate the defeated opponent.

As a survival technique, Buck invested in his dog and his horse qualities which in more normal times would have been reserved for the important people in his life.

In summary, the main character in this book, Buck, lives in extraordinary times and does his best to be true to his values while events swirl around him over which he has no control. The microcosm of his life in his military unit becomes a major element in his growth into manhood. The author succeeds in bringing into focus one individual's journey, both physically and spiritually, which causes him to become a far different person than he was at the outset. This is a story which will appeal to readers of different ages and varied backgrounds.

By

Dr. Donald P. Hines: PHD—Police Psychologist; Retired from the Guam Police Department. Dr. Hines furnished creative ideas and wonderful support to Smoky Mountain Roots. He was much involved in a previous novel by Fortner, "The Shiny Badge", sharing his psychological training, experiences, and insight in portraying an accurate psychological profile and report on a major character in the book.

Major Marcus Miller, Company G 62nd North Carolina
Regiment
Sandy Shepherd Artist, Westfield Massachusetts

CHAPTER ONE
Smoky Mountain Roots

It was cold as hell when he stumbled on the body just before daylight about three miles back in the swamp. His hands burned with the cold. It was not yet dawn, but the breaking light out of the East promised a clear day. He had been very quiet when he heard one shot from a rifle. It echoed across the valley and ricocheted off the trees, then bounced back down from the mountains.

Now he was alert, but not yet apprehensive, just assuming it was another hunter. Still he wondered how they could see in such dim light. God, it was cold. He rubbed his hands together and wiped his nose on the back of his sleeve.

As he walked he heard the rubbing of the denim as he took each step. His brogans were split in places. He had rubbed them good with hog lard, and they felt soft.

As he leaned over to tie his shoe, his shoulder and back muscles bulged. He wore his hair long, but not tied, and wore a slouch hat much the worse for wear.

His eyes were enough to scare the devil out of an observer. They were a slate color and clear as a spring. Not a large youth, but one could tell that Buck Roland would grow into a heck of a man. Right now he was scared because this was the first time he had seen a dead man except at a funeral.

He instinctively knew the man was dead, and to make it doubly scary, he turned the body over and gazed into wide-open glazed eyes. He saw that the man was the father of a family enemy, the father of three boys around the age of Buck. The two families had been feuding for several years. The disagreement came about when Buck's father purchased a fifty acre piece of land that had been coveted by the deceased, Joe Daniels.

Buck recognized the body and shuddered as he looked into the face of death. A rifle shot had caught Joe between his eyes, splattering blood on the checkered reddened black shirt as it drained from the bullet wound. Daniels' squirrel rifle lay in the grass nearby. One overall gallus was undone and he had been shot while he had just finished doing his business. "This really smells," Buck thought.

He quickly checked the man's neck for a pulse, and finding no sign of life decided to make his way to the family cabin by running the shortest and quickest way. Cold as it was he waded through the creek and within thirty minutes was in calling distance of his home.

A log cabin, obviously built some years ago, had been added too as the Roland family increased in size. The cabin was in the North Carolina Appalachian Mountains. The Appalachian Mountain range, located in Eastern North America, extends from South Quebec to North Alabama, roughly 1600 miles.

The Appalachian Trail is a hiking trail from Maine to North Georgia along the Appalachian Mountains.

The Blue Ridge Mountains are described thusly due to their bluish appearance in the distance. They are the easternmost range of the Appalachians, stretching from Southern Pennsylvania to North Georgia.

The Black Mountains (an American Indian descriptive name) are the highest range of the Appalachians in West

North Carolina, and is a branch of the Blue Ridge Mountains of which the highest peak is Mt. Mitchell.

He began yelling at the top of his lungs, and the door of the cabin was flung wide. His mother came to meet him. He wondered why his father and his brother and sister did not appear.

He excitedly stammered out, "Ma, there is going to be hell to pay. Joe Daniels has been murdered. I know they will blame me. You know Zeke and his brothers jumped me, and I whipped them with a stick. Their father swore he would do me in after that happened. You know Pa tried to talk to him, but he wouldn't listen. Ma, I swear I didn't kill him. I found him already dead, shot between the eyes. Where is Pa?"

"He went to get a load of wood. Get that Buckskin mare out of the lot and ride as fast as you can to where he is cutting wood. Then let him go after the sheriff while you come back home where I can see you."

Buck did not think of questioning his Ma. He jumped on the mare and left running. He rode fast and dangerously to the area where he knew his father always cut wood.

When he told his pa, Leon Roland, what had happened, his pa said, "They will try to blame this killing on you. Did you see or hear anything else?"

Buck was steadfast in repeating what he had already told was the total truth.

Leon said, "I believe you son. Go on back to your ma and don't leave her side. Don't open the door for nobody. I will go get the law."

Buck trudged back to the cabin with grave forebodings about his being blamed for this dirty deed. "I may have to run for it," he thought.

His mind was a jungle. He previously had plans to find

a wife, get a piece of this mountain, and raise a family. He didn't want his family to have to go through the anguish of the renewed feud with the Daniels bunch. They would surely try to take the life of a Roland because of the enmity between the Roland and the Daniels' clans.

While he and his ma waited, they talked of various things they might do to avoid another death between the families. When Buck told her he might have to run, she trembled and was no longer able to hold back her tears, telling him there might be other ways.

He knew that he and his pa would have to make this decision, because they knew the way of things in the mountains.

It was just not the land causing the feud. There had been a multitude of reasons that the Daniels did not trust the Roland's. One of the major reasons was that Daniels was a dyed in the wool moon-shiner, while the Roland's were strictly law abiding folk.

The Roland clan was steeped too the bone with their mother's insistence that they all go to church regularly and stay straight, as she described it.

Once a relative of theirs had actually told the sheriff where a Daniels still was located. When Daniels got out of jail he had promptly, with the help of several other Daniels, broken the informant's leg and almost killed him.

In his own heart Buck knew what he had to do. How he would do it he did not know yet. He was not afraid; he just didn't want to endanger his family.

This was late in the month of June, 1862. This morning when he got up to go squirrel hunting it was still dark. He took his pa's little squirrel dog, Tige, with him because his own dog, Orso, had to be chained to a barn post because a plow line wouldn't hold him. Hunting squirrels with Orso would have been like taking an ox for transportation to church.

Buck, a very sociable youth, was friends with the Cherokee youths who lived about five miles down the valley on the creek. Buck was a good wrestler, and the Indian youths had been trying to best him for years. Buck had stopped a group of white boys from bothering a group of young Indians. Since then he could come and go on the Cherokee village as a trusted friend.

He never bothered the girls, and spent his time with the Indian boys his own age. He learned to speak a little Cherokee and taught them some elementary English, (mountain variety). In turn, they let him ride their ponies and horses and play in their games.

Buck was still in his formative years at age fifteen. He was strong and quick, and could hold his temper even while he was putting forth his stuff to win. He could even laugh when they played a joke on him or got the best of him. He could hold his own. Even the old elders looked upon "Stone Eyes", as they called him, favorably. They had even talked in the Council of letting him go up the mountain on the climb to become a man. He had never done it yet, but he wanted to. Running Wolf, his best Indian friend, was supposed to go this winter.

During this growing up period in the mountains, his pa, Buck, and brother, Luke, hunted hogs for the family smoke house. These feral hogs made good meat and sausage. It was also a great sport with the mountaineers as it was dangerous and exciting.

Their hog dogs would catch and hold the hogs and his pa would shoot the porker, which would sometimes weigh as much as two or three hundred pounds. On one of these hunts they caught a sow, weighing about two hundred pounds which had a young suckling piglet boar still with her.

Buck talked his pa into letting him take the little boar home to raise, in a pen. The Indian boys came over to see the little wild boar and set about getting him from Buck as a breeding boar.

Buck had obtained Orso as a puppy. The Indians had somehow obtained Orso from some Chinese men migrating through the North Carolina Mountains. So Buck traded the little boar pig for the Alaskan malamute pup in an even trade. Buck's friend, Running Wolf, told him the puppy's name was Orso.

Orso was now about nine months old and was still growing. He followed Buck everywhere, except squirrel hunting. He was a good feral hog dog. He could hold any size hog without much effort. He usually took the hog's whole snout in his mouth, and just sat down and waited until Leon could shoot the hog.

It was funny. Buck had been told by some of the old mountain men that Orso would probably weigh over one hundred fifty pounds when he was grown. The Daniels' boys had a bull dog about seventy-five pounds named Killer. Killer had whipped all the bad dogs in the mountains round about the valley.

One day Buck and Orso were heading to the Indian camp and ran into the Daniels brothers and their fighting bull dog, Killer. Ole Killer was foaming at the mouth from the get go to do battle with Orso. Orso appeared uninterested and paid Killer no mind until Killer tried to go for Orso's throat. Finally Orso got mad. He ran into Killer, knocked him down, put both of his front feet on Killer's chest, and took his entire muzzle in his jaws. Orso sat there and shook that bull dog until he was senseless. He then pushed him away and walked over to Buck as if to say, "Let's go."

Buck walked away with Orso without looking back. All the while the Daniels brothers were shouting obscenities and cursing at them. Buck knew right then that he had him a first class fighting dog. Orso really didn't care.

It was nearly dark when his pa and Sheriff Garrison Patrick came to the Roland cabin. The sheriff was well aware of bad feelings between the Roland and the Daniels' clans. He knew it really amounted too a feud, and in the mountains this meant generations of hatred, spiteful acts, and other things often leading too a killing or a murder.

The sheriff reluctantly and solemnly informed the Roland's that Buck had to be put in jail to keep the Daniels boys from killing him.

Buck called his pa aside and told him, "I will go to jail and tonight you bring the Buckskin mare, Gay Lady, Orso, a few clothes, a slicker, a sack of food, and twenty-five dollars for the jailor, Moe Miller, who is the sheriff's cousin, and bring a few dollars for me. I will run. I can tell you now, pa, I am going to join the Confederate troops up in Jackson County. I think I can get into the Infantry, and be a scout. I want to fight, and I am tired of those Yankees killing our boys."

Buck's father knew the jailer and from previous experience knew that twenty-five dollars would give his beloved son a chance to get away.

The sheriff would be relieved of the odious task of trying to keep Buck alive while he was trying to run the real killer down. Philosophically, he knew that Buck Roland had not killed Joe Daniels. He even had a good idea who did it.

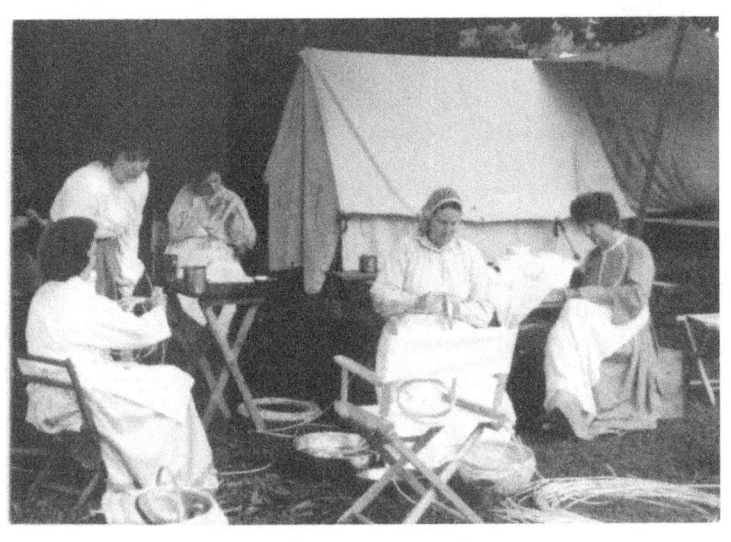

CORINA LEARNS BASKET WEAVING

CHAPTER TWO
A Girl Named Corina

Along about ten that night, Buck was sitting in the log jail talking to Moe about dogs and hunting. He had eaten a great meal of greens, cornbread, and buttermilk. He and Moe ate together from Moe's supper his wife had brought for him and Buck.

She hugged Buck and said, "Son, I know you didn't do that." After she left, Buck was half dozing when he heard the soft whippoorwill signal his pa could do so well.

Buck handed Moe an envelope his pa had passed through the shuttered window. Moe casually stuck the envelope in his hip pocket, stretched long and hard and mumbled, "Boy, I'm going to lie down in the back. Keep quiet now."

Buck slipped easily out the open window and felt his father's hand on his shoulder. They made their way to the mare tied deep in the woods.

Orso was tied to the same tree, and wonder of all wonders, was quiet as he could be. Buck knew Orso sensed the need for quiet and wanted to please them.

Buck was given the things he had asked for and was pleased and surprised when his pa gave him his own highly prized Dixie Sharps 1859 Military Rifle. There were approximately 115,000 of these carbines made during the Civil War. They were favored by the Calvary and the Infantry by both the North and the South and were associated mostly with sharpshooters.

No one had touched this rifle but his father, since he brought it home without any explanation. It had been well used, but not abused.

His father refused to discuss its origin. Speculation had it that one of the rogue Roland's, in a fit of rebellion, had joined the Union Army and for a short time had fought against the South.

He came to his senses, wanted back in his own roots, deserted the Army and returned to the valley. He gave the rifle to Leon Roland so that it would not identify him as a deserter and as a traitor to the South.

Leon Roland was a staunch supporter of the South's cause, but was able to accept the rebel back because he knew that the Civil War was a many headed monster. By the same token he knew that Buck would, without a second thought, join the Southerners nearby.

Leon and Buck hugged good-bye. Buck mounted the mare, Gay Lady, untied Orso, but kept him tied on a rope to the saddletree and headed off into the night. Unbeknownst to his pa, Buck had two stops to make before he started to run for his life.

Lucy Morgan, Corina Daniels cousin, had come by the jail with a message for Buck from Corina, daughter of the dead man. Corina was brief. She wrote, "Give the whippoorwill signal and I will come out. Be very quiet and careful; they are all in a killing mood."

After he had seen Corina, he would stop by the hollow tree his clan kept for messages, money, or anything they wanted to keep a secret. A member of the Roland bunch checked this regularly and the message they would leave there for his pa would be quickly and quietly delivered.

When he arrived at the Daniels' property he tied the mare

and Orso, and prayed that Gay Lady would not rub the bridle off and that Orso would continue to be quiet.

He crept to the end of the paling fenced yard where he knew Corina slept near the window. Buck was wet with sweat from fear, but bravely gave the signal.

Buck thought he heard Corona's feet hit the floor and he nearly wet his pants. Then he saw her wraith-like figure slide out of the window. He knew he heard her feet hit the hard dirt and just about fainted when Daniels' old hound padded up to Corina without making a sound.

Lo and behold, Corina had handed the hound a big piece of cornbread which he took greedily and went under the house to eat.

By this time Corina had slipped through a hole where a paling was missing, and Buck had her by the hand. He led her into the woods until he thought they were safe. He spread his shirt on the ground and they immediately locked up.

Corina was sixteen and a virgin. Her pa, old man Daniels, was so fierce and protective that all the neighborhood boys were scared, and so was Corina. She was a pretty girl and by today's standards she would be called beautiful. Full figured for her age she was also blessed with flawless pink skin, dark intelligent eyes, and thick dark hair. She tied her hair back pony-tailed-like, and when she tossed her head, Buck's heart always jumped.

Buck told her he was going to join up and when he got out of the army he would come for her, since he would be on the run, and take her out of the mountains for good.

As they lay together their physical need for each other was such that they were trembling. Buck knew she had never done it, and told her he was willing to wait until they got married. He did tell her that he was as hot as a fresh fired mini ball. He was taken totally by surprise when he felt between her legs and encountered long silken hair and no pants. He gasped when his hand reached the promise land, finding it deliciously wet and ready. By now he knew it was too late, and rolled on top of her. She choked back a sob of pain as he entered her, but right away said, "Go ahead." After a short while she cried, "It don't hurt no more" and pleaded, "Love me Buck and show me how."

Buck had gotten his sex education from a pretty widow in the valley. She was about thirty-five years old, and taught the class to all the mountain boys. There were few virginal boys in the area due to her generous nature, which was serve one-serve all. They all thought she was a nymphomaniac.

When Buck asked the widow if she would give Flying Wolf a little, she laughed and said, "Why not?"

When Buck and Corina finished, they knew they were truly in love and would one day be married. Corina knew who killed her daddy, and therefore, the accusation against Buck would not hold up.

Their parting was tearful, and they were both crying. Buck finally kissed her good-bye and snuck away to his mare and his dog.

He rode his faithful horse to the hollow tree. Buck wrote his pa he would get word to him and, send the mare home. Buck would decide what to do with Orso after he was in the army and see if he could keep him. He assured his family he would be alright, and asked them not to try to reach him and to burn this note under the wash pot.

He rode out of the valley, and as he looked back he felt like his world had ended. The future was unknown and scary. He had little education, although he could read and write a little. Buck knew that physically he could take anything the army threw at him. He really looked forward to some action to take his mind off his troubles.

Buck had heard about Yankee Forces committing atrocities on the families of some southerners, and was consumed with a passion to try to even up the score. He knew he could ride, shoot and fight, and he knew he would be scared, but could go ahead and get the job done. Buck had never killed a person, but he knew that in battle he would be able to kill without any trepidation.

He rode all night, mostly through Indian trails in Jackson County's Indian Nation. Sylva, North Carolina, in Jackson County, has the Tuckasegee River as one of its natural beauty areas. He saw three Indians coming straight toward him from the river looking very grim. Buck smiled and said the conventional Cherokee word for good morning. They were surprised, and asked him for his name.

"I am Stone Eyes."

They laughed and said, "Running Wolf claims that you could out wrestle us. Where are you going?"

"I must confess I am a little bit lost."

They turned their ponies around and guided him up a winding rocky trail that almost went straight up. This trail lasted to the top of the mountain rise, and as they came to the top they stopped their ponies and each of them in turn gave him a little gift.

One gave him a handful of pemmican, one gave him a handful of greens, and one gave him a bunch of wild onions. He could eat for at least a day or two with these gifts.

Buck raised his right hand toward them as he pulled his mare around. They pointed to Orso, and said, "Bear, a male because I saw his old thing hanging out." They laughed heartily and took off down the mountain sliding and jumping.

It was a good show and Buck felt better. He knew that Flying Wolf would get the word that he was hiding out, and would know that he had not forsaken his Indian friends. He still kept Orso tied to the McClellan saddle tree to make sure they did not get separated.

He saw smoke in the distance and realized he was getting far away from his own neighborhood. This was for him, unchartered parts of the mountain.

As he came within looking distance of a home spread he saw a family moving around the place. The woman had a bonnet on, bending over a steaming wash pot stirring clothes.

Near the barn a man was trying to shoe a horse. A boy of about ten or twelve was no help and the horse was about to get the best of his father.

A couple of cows were in the pen ready to be milked. Their calves were outside the pens lowing and bellowing loudly.

Orso finally gave a bark that must have sounded like a roar of thunder to the family. The man dropped the line from the horse, the tools from his hands, grabbed his son, and raced toward the crib where there was a rifle leaning against the door. He got it and turned full toward Buck hollering, "Stop there boy, or I will have to put one in you."

Buck knew what to do answering, "Sir, I am from over Sylva way on my way to join up. I mean you and your family no harm. I would like to feed and water my horse, feed my dog, and sleep in your barn tonight."

"Come on up slow."

About this time the ugliest hound dog Buck had ever seen came from around the barn. He was the right color for a hound, but there the resemblance stopped. His head was small; about the size of a feist dog, he had a bob tail, and was fat as a butterball.

Orso merely looked at him and shook his head. He didn't even bark; he just grunted and sat down. Buck asked if he could get down, and the settler, Jones, agreed.

The boy was peeping around from the back of his father. The woman came up and said, "What's the ruckus about?"

She was as pretty as a picture. Buck thought she didn't come from around here.

They readily saw Buck as trustworthy and that Orso was not into fighting their dog whose name was "Nothing."

Buck was invited to eat with them and told he could sleep in the barn. They were excited to see a stranger. Buck said, "Mr. Jones let's shoe that horse before we do anything else."

Jones replied, "If you know how, let's get it done."

Buck knew how because his pa had taught him. He showed Jones how to tie up the leg that was being shod so that if the horse reared around he would fall. Then he rasped the split hoof, filed a ragged edge off straight and smooth and then asked for a shoe. He took it to a chopping block and pounded it straight. Buck then took the hoof nails from a box and nailed the shoe on nice and straight with a building hammer. Buck straightened up, rubbed his back and said, "If the job is alright, Mr. Jones I am hungry."

Mrs. Jones said, "Give me a few minutes while you stow your gear; then come on and wash for supper."

The little boy, named Joshua, had thawed out by now and was talking a mile a minute.

After supper Mr. Jones said, "Son, you can join up with the 62nd Regiment, Company G in Waynesville, North Carolina. My brother, Maxwell Jones, is in Company G. He is a mounted scout and works with a man called an artificer. He smiled and said, "Max can help you get started. It is about twenty-five miles of rough country to get there."

Buck had already won the hearts of the Jones family. They could not do enough for him.

The next morning, Buck, with Orso in tow, and astride Gay Lady was about five miles toward Waynesville when Jones got up. Mr. Jones found a piece of hard rock sugar, wrapped in a clean cloth, for Joshua. Buck left a note saying, "This is all I had for Joshua. If you ever need me, holler."

The going was rough, but Buck rode steadily and only slept a few hours. By mid afternoon of the next day he hailed the sentry on duty at the Infantry post at Waynesville.

He had ridden Gay Lady twenty-five miles in two days. Buck had only stopped briefly to eat from his poke and feed Orso and Gay Lady. They were all wet, scratched, dirty, thirsty, and hungry.

SENTRY DUTY

CHAPTER THREE
The 62nd North Carolina Infantry

The sentry growled and said, "Where in the hell did you come from?"

Buck answered pleasantly, "I want to join up."

The sentry told him to turn Gay Lady in with the other infantry horses. "Tie that monster to that pole over there. We don't usually have no dogs here, they are too noisy. Bed down in that tent over there. I know there is an empty cot because junior got himself killed. In the morning go to Captain Miller's quarters and tell him you want to enlist."

Orso was tired. He ate his cornbread, drank his water, and promptly went to sleep.

Buck woke up the next morning to the smell of wood smoke and bacon frying. "Lordy that food smells good." He went to see about Orso and noticed he had been fed and watered as the friendly stable hands had been feeding and watering the horses.

Gay Lady, a quiet friendly horse, was already accepted. One of the stable hands, a private from Waynesville, said, "Boy, don't you know that mare is with foal?" Buck was astonished and said, "No Sir, I didn't."

"Yep, sure is, and don't call me Sir. I am a private. If you see a sergeant's stripes or some rank showing him to be an officer, then it is time to say Sir."

Buck was learning. The private sent him to the mess tent

and pointed out Captain Miller's office. "Go there after you eat."

Buck was excited. He saw a bunch of Cherokee Indians bustling around like soldiers on his way to the Captain's office. He spoke friendly to the Cherokees in their own language. They took this as a measure of respect and answered him in Cherokee. They talked to themselves pointing at him and wondering who he was.

After breakfast Captain Miller was behind his desk talking to three grizzled infantry men; a Sergeant Major, Jack Parker, an Artificer, named Cogburn, and a young white scout named Maxwell Jones.

Buck noticed that Jones was a focal figure in the conversation. They asked Jones directions to where a bunch of outlaws were, and they asked how many he figured there were.

The military had been asked to chase down, capture or kill a bunch of deserters. They were outlaws, renegades, and rapists who made the mistake of coming near Waynesville.

Captain Miller said, "Max, can you find them again?"

"Yes Sir, I'll need a day or two and a man to ride with me."

Miller then turned to Buck and said, "Son, what can I do for you?"

Miller's steely eyes and stern visage softened because he was thinking this is a likely looking boy about the age of my own son. Captain Miller's son was killed in a battle two days before.

Buck almost shouted, "I want to join up Sir," as he jumped up and saluted.

Captain Miller smiled and said, "You brought a horse and a monster dog with you."

"Yes Sir, it is my pa's horse and my little old Alaskan Malamute, Orso."

Captain Miller replied, "You don't know size very well," and smiled.

Buck said, "I ain't got no education. I can read and write some. I shoot good. I know some Cherokee Indian talk—I know the mountains and how to move quiet. I am a good squirrel hunter."

Miller's grin was wide as he handed Buck a set of papers and said, "Sign up. You know you will have to send that dog and that pregnant mare out of here pronto."

"I will Sir, I promise you. I will send them or take them to my pa."

The Sergeant Major helped him with the enlistment papers and told him to report to Maxwell Jones for training and duty.

It was Maxwell's eighteen year old scout partner, Junior Cooper, who was killed three days before by a renegade sniper. This was the same bunch of animals that Maxwell was directed to go back and find and pinpoint for Miller's troops and the Cherokee Indians. Miller's comment was, "We will capture or kill them before we quit."

When Buck and Maxwell left the Captain's quarters, Buck was stepping high. Buck was now a private in the 62nd Regiment, Company G, and was going to be a scout. Hot dam, he was happy. He never gave a thought to the possibility of getting killed. He lay down on Junior Cooper's cot and then it dawned on him. "I am in a dead mans bed and I am going out to do the same job."

For awhile this dulled his sense of relief at getting into the army so quick. He drifted off to sleep dreaming of Corina.

He knew he loved her dearly. He pondered, "Will she wait on me?"

"God a mighty, are we in a mountain slide?"

Buck found himself flying off the cot and crashing into the wall in a clatter of gear and weapons. He woke up and thought he was having a nightmare. A shaved headed brute was getting him by the collar and began dragging him outside the tent.

This big, dirty trooper threw Buck in the dirt, spit on him and said, "You was in Junior's bed."

Buck, dazed, shook his head and finally got to his feet. Luckily, Maxwell Jones ran up and said, "Hondo, the boy did not mean no harm. The sentry told him where to sleep last night." Hondo was a former circus wrestler and regiment bully. No one in the regiment had been able to whip him.

Maxwell sat down in the dirt with Buck, wiped him off and said, "You know you will have to fight him or you will never make it here." Maxwell continued, "After he whips you he will leave you alone. Until you fight him you will have no peace from him or the other men."

Maxwell sighed and said, "Shit, there ain't no other way."

Captain Miller, a fair and just man, knew all about this. He told Maxwell to arrange a fight between the two after they returned from the patrol. "It is to be a sporting event which will create a diversion for the men and get this thing out of the way."

CHAPTER FOUR
The Mountains Turn Red

Maxwell was very surprised when he and Buck were talking about the upcoming fight with Hondo. Buck said, "I was going to fight him anyway. I am not scared of him."

The reason he felt this way was because he had been taught every trick of fighting the Indians knew. He was unusually strong for his size, and loved to fight for fun. He seldom fought in anger. This made him a cool adversary. His secret weapon was the fighting sessions taught by his pa, deep in the woods.

Several times his pa had said, "Son, your good nature is going to get you killed sometime."

Before Buck knew what was happening, his pa had him on the ground with a knee in his back, one of his arms pulled around behind him until it was almost to the breaking point, and a rough stick drawing it across his throat.

"See there, if this was a knife you would be dead already."

Later on Buck had found that his father was an experienced fighter. He solemnly, and somewhat shyly, told Buck, "I have not always been quiet and laid back like I am now. I had to do a lot of things to get here and protect your ma and my family. I never told you this before, but I even had to put a whipping on Joe Daniels way back when we first got here. This was the real reason our feud began. I broke his nose and his collar bone.

I have had to watch my back all these years. When you found the body of ole Joe Daniels, I really was not surprised that someone had killed the ole sumbitch."

Buck never told anyone about these confidences. He never told anyone how his pa taught him to be a dirty fighter.

Maxwell Jones was a little older than Buck. He was a happy, unassuming mountain boy. He loved horses, was friendly and at home in the woods. He also liked the Cherokees, although he was not raised with them.

Word spread around the compound that Hondo was going to whip the new scout the day after they came back from the patrol.

Buck and Maxwell went to the horse lot. Maxwell pointed out three horses. "Take your pick for your own scout horse."

Buck walked into the corral. He wanted to check the horses' legs, hooves, fetlocks, and chests. He looked deep into each of the horses' eyes. He finally backed off and said, "Maxwell, that gray looking horse with the wavy mane is mine".

Maxwell laughed and said, "One of the Cherokees brought him in on a halter and nobody has put a saddle on him yet. He looks like a Mustang to me. He is a mite small, but you ain't all that heavy and all he will have to carry is you, your knapsack, a carbine, your long knife and your ammo. He may be big enough."

Buck went to the left side of his chosen horse and shoved a lump of sugar in his mouth. He whispered, "Cody, you are mine."

Cody knocked his hand away with his nose and some of that sugar taste got on his nose. He had never tasted sweets before. Cody turned toward Buck, who extended his hand, and low and behold Cody got the entire chunk this time.

Maxwell supplied some more rock sugar and slipped it

to Buck. When he came back in one hour, Cody was standing spraddle-legged with a halter and a saddle blanket on his back. Buck was singing a lullaby to the horse. Cody and Buck were bonding.

Hurrying the process, he knew he had to get in the saddle soon. Normally, he would have taken a couple of weeks to train a new horse.

Making it harder, Hondo, the ugly sergeant, heckled Buck and said, "Don't worry about riding that horse because when I get through with you, you won't be able to ride or walk."

When Hondo approached Orso for the first time, Orso made a noise that was hideous to hear and came to the end of his leash. The hair on his neck was straight up and his eyes turned red with hate. His mouth was so huge that in a fight with a bull dog his entire muzzle was in Orso's mouth. Orso bared his awesome teeth.

Hondo shouted, "I am going to have to kill that thing."

Buck silently said, "You will have to kill me first."

Hondo left the area in full flight. He went crazy when the other troopers laughed at him.

Buck started handling Cody all over, leading him with the halter and a blanket on his back. He then eased the McClellan Saddle on his back.

Cody promptly dumped the saddle by darting side ways. Buck quietly picked up the blanket and saddle and did it all over again. Cody tired of this game and stood quiet as a mouse.

Buck led him around the circular training lot without dislodging the saddle. Buck took Cody to the holding post and gave him a carrot.

While Cody was occupied, Buck slowly tightened the

saddle girth. The horse became nervous, but he was led around the circle anyway. Now it was time for Buck to get aboard.

Buck got the halter rope in one hand and quick as a cat was in the saddle. Cody bowed his neck, arched his back, and was ready to really put on a bucking show. Buck leaned over and stuffed a carrot in the side of his mouth and started humming in his ear.

Cody didn't know whether to fart, shit, or go blind. He was beginning to like this guy. This guy who never hurt him, made sweet sounds, no threatening moves, and was always giving him something good to eat.

Cody eased up on his coiled muscles and let out a big fart, as if to say, I am still a man-horse. What is it you want? Buck laughed out loud.

Buck knew it was time for the ultimate test, by getting on and off the saddle on Cody's back. He was on Cody's left side, the correct side for mounting and when he put his foot in the stirrup, Cody just moved away, leaving Buck helplessly spraddled. This wouldn't work.

Next time Buck put his weight in the stirrup, and swung swiftly into the saddle. It would have been a perfect mount except the saddle girth was loosely tied, which allowed the saddle to go under Cody's belly.

Cody started bucking. It would have been bad, but Cody took care not to jump on Buck who was sitting in the dirt.

Finally, with carrots, Buck coaxed Cody to stop. Cody was trembling with fear and excitement. He settled down and this time Buck properly tightened the saddle in place.

After being fed the carrots, it seemed Cody said to himself, "This is fun."

Buck was in the saddle like greased lightning. The horse took about eight or nine crow hops because he thought it was expected of him. He was puzzled when Buck started singing lullabies again. It was over.

In another hour Cody was saddle broken with his spirit in-tact the way it was supposed to be. The other soldiers had never seen a horse broken so easy and so gentle. Buck knew horses. Max Jones said, "Buck, we need to talk."

"Can I bring my horse?"

"Oh; Yea."

They sat on a log and Max recounted the losses of men and how much the infantry depended on the scout's information, and how dangerous the job was.

He went over the fact that the Captain's son had been killed and that Captain Miller was taken with Buck. "We can't let him down. Leave your Sharps rifle here. I am going to get you a shotgun. Put all your gear on Cody and start riding through the woods, away from the regiment for one hour. Don't shoot me because I am going to find you."

Without a question, Buck rode, twisting and turning through the brush of the mountains, climbing about a half a mile high.

He tied Cody to a Juniper and hid behind a boulder. Here he waited silently. About an hour later Max dropped a rock on his head from the top of the boulder. Maxwell Jones was quite a scout. He could easily have shot Buck from above.

Max explained how he accomplished this feat and laconically said, "Lesson number one. Don't let the enemy find you, you find him."

Buck liked his teacher. Maxwell then dropped the fact that they would leave before daylight tomorrow. "I will wake you myself and put nothing on your horse or your person that makes any noise. Here is some leather grease. Use it on your gear until you can get on and off your horse without even a leather squeak. Clean your shotgun and get all your ammo ready. Take rations and water for one day. They will have to last you for two days."

Buck prepared his saddle, shotgun, scabbard, knife and sheath, as instructed by Max. He had gotten off and on Cody so much until he was sure there was no noise. (Cody was a natural). He walked quietly and being a gelding he did not whicker as much as a stud. A gentle hand on his mouth would silence him every time. Buck slept hard until Max handed him a cup of coffee and a piece of hardtack. He said, "I'll meet you at the stable."

They got their horses ready and Buck said, "Old Cody, are you ready?"

He took Orso a piece of hardtack and a bucket of water. Miraculously, Orso was quiet.

They rode in tandem when they could, keeping off the roads and trails. While they were riding, Max told him that Junior was killed because they had stumbled on the renegades. Before they had time to take cover, Junior was killed by a renegade sniper. He had a fatal wound in the chest. Max hid nearby until the outlaws decided Junior was alone and went back to the spring.

"THE BLUE SUITS"
"The Union"—A Formidable Enemy

They took Junior's horse and left his body. Max crawled to Junior and patiently dragged him back to his own horse. Max put Junior behind his saddle. It was a long ride back to camp. This was sobering information for Buck.

They were already about ten miles from the regiment when they smelled smoke and heard some quiet talking. Snipers would be out, but Max and Buck had to get close enough to get an estimate of how many of the enemy they had to fight or subdue. They also had to check out the terrain.

It was a sinkhole with a clear spring in the middle of a ravine. They looked down on the camp, lying on their bellies without talking. There were at least five hundred Union men, horses and guns. They had a Gat-ling gun and were well armed. They were better equipped than the Infantry. Although well dressed and well equipped they had no particular uniform. The intrepid scouts had seen enough.

As they were crawling backwards, always away from the spring, they heard someone walking toward them. Buck said, "Lord Jesus, it is a sniper who was asleep when we crawled in."

Buck rolled up in the grass and Max hid himself behind a tall pine tree. The sniper was wiping sleep from his eyes when Max killed him by driving his bayonet clean through him.

Max eased the enemy to the ground and whispered to Buck, "We got to hide him."

They hid him, covering his body with stone, grass, and leaves. When they got back to the horses, Buck was awash with sweat, which actually stank because of his fear.

Maxwell was pretty cool, and said very little on the ride back to camp, which was in very rough country. They had observed the enemy group was capable and ready to fight. They reported to Captain Miller that they believed the raid was, "Now or never."

The sniper they killed would very certainly be missed. Even if they did not find his body he would be missed at roll call.

Miller called his leaders together and told them to get ready to march within the hour. He sent Buck to tell the Cherokees to get ready. They were told to get weapons, food, and water for two days.

The Cherokees really wanted to fight because they knew it was only a matter of time before the renegades would be all over their nation. They were willing fighters for their own people. They liked the good food, and they were given a little money and tobacco by the military. They really believed the military would return the favor and fight for them in their tribal wars. They were grossly misled.

Captain Miller's strategy was to come in on three sides of the camp at the spring, and trap them. This would give his troops a big advantage because they would be firing down upon their surprised enemy instead of on a level or looking up. It all depended on a quiet arrival. Quiet would be hard to maintain with four hundred soldiers and three hundred Indians. Buck thought with all this noise, it won't be much of a surprise.

The surprise came when Miller told him, "You, Max and the Indians wait a safe distance from the enemy camp. You will be in the raid with the Indians and the Infantry on the West side."

Buck took a shotgun, pistol, long rifle, and his knife with him as they made their way around the spring where they waited several hours for the other two units to get in place. To Buck's ears all this movement sounded like a thundering herd.

Lieutenant, Regis Phillips, was in charge of the ground forces, aided by a sergeant. When the Lieutenant arrived on the scene, he called to Max, "Lead on Mac Beth." Captain Miller told me, "When the shooting begins anyone on horses would come down the hillside, ride into the battle, and finish up. Just be dammed sure you don't shoot your own troops."

Fifty soldiers were mixed with one hundred fifty Indians. Another group was composed the same. They were told to get as close to the camp as possible from the two opposite sides.

When the first shot sounded, they were to make their run on the enemy as fast as possible. They were ordered to throw caution and quietness aside. "Don't stop until the enemy surrenders. Don't worry about the cost," they were told.

Max, by now, had tied his horse and was on foot, loaded down with his weapons and gear. He was well aware that the enemy would have to be stone deaf not to be ready for their attack. He knew his job was to stay ahead of his Indians, and run as fast as he could toward the enemy, until they were engaged hand to hand.

Their weapons were on ready. Their move toward the spring had begun. "Oh Shit," a private stumbled and accidentally fired his weapon. All hell broke loose.

Max kept running ahead of his mixed troops. The Indians were making their blood curdling battle cries. It was pandemonium, no time to think, only one thing to do. Keep running for the spring.

All of a sudden a disorganized bunch of the outlaws rose up and began shooting at them point blank. In return fire about an equal number from both sides were killed or wounded. Then they were fighting hand to hand. Buck saw a Cherokee being throttled by a big outlaw. The Indian was turning blue and gasping his last breaths. Quick as a cougar, Buck was behind the outlaw, pulled his head back, slit his throat, and pushed him to the ground.

In the throes of dying the outlaw was a ghastly sight. His blood had gushed all over Buck and the Indian. Without saying anything to each other, Buck and the Indian jumped back into the fight.

All of Miller's forces were in the arena, and there was much screaming as men were wounded and killed. The few mounted soldiers were using their sabers well and viciously. The outlaws were good fighters and were fighting for their lives.

Buck felt a stinging in his shoulder and felt blood running down his side. His assailant was still coming for him. Buck pretended to fall, but halfway down, wheeled and plunged his knife into the enemy's chest. He must have hit a main artery because blood pumped out of him.

The renegade shouted, "You sumbitch you have kilt me," and fell to the ground.

Suddenly a white flag was raised by the commander of the renegade force. Buck looked skyward and said, "Thank you Lord Jesus."

Captain Miller shouted, "Cease fire, secure the prisoners and tend to the wounded. It is over." They had killed thirty-five Confederates and ten horses. Captain Miller's soldiers had killed two hundred of the enemy. This was a resounding victory.

Buck was still on his feet, but he was weak and feeling sick to his stomach. He had just killed two men close up, and he had lost count of how many he had killed with his rifle, shotgun and pistol. He knew he would never be the same Buck Roland again. When the Doctor, Aman Summers, saw him retching and bleeding he tended his wounds by sanitizing them and sewing up the gash in Buck's shoulder. Outside of being painful there was no real damage to Buck's person. The only damage was to his thoughts and emotions. His great solace was that he had been fighting for his life.

CHAPTER 5
The Grudge Fight

When the outlaws were killed and the other criminals were reduced to submission, Captain Miller was faced with the problem of disposing of the prisoners. The closest Confederate Civil War Prison for Union soldiers was at Salisbury, North Carolina. This was one hundred fifty-eight miles west of Waynesville.

The Cherokee Indians and the Infantry, capable of duty, were assigned to march the prisoners to Salisbury for holding.

Buck and Max found and roped their unharmed horses that were wandering loose with many of the outlaw horses. Cody had only sustained a gash on his left flank which was not severe.

They were ordered to return these horses to the regiment and to kill any of the horses that could not be saved. All this blood, including the hand to hand killing of two fellow human beings, convinced Buck that an army career was not what he wanted. He would stick it out as long as he could because he believed the South was right.

Several days went by, spent in restoring a semblance of order to the chaos which had been created. Miller, an orderly competent officer, set about establishing a chain of command both efficient and loyal.

Buck relished the fact that Orso was alright, but realized that Orso could not remain with the regiment. The same with Gay Lady—they had to go home.

Also bearing on his mind was the fight between him and Hondo. He knew he had to get ready. His shoulder was a little sore, but would soon be well.

Cody was surprising calm. His initiation to battle only resulted in the slight wound, which was nearly well with no crippling effect. Cody was now a full blown veteran Infantry Mount.

Cody was now completely bonded with Buck. He would leave the other horses and come to meet Buck anywhere. Because Cody was a gelding, he was not a trouble maker with the other horses, unless he was put in with the stallions and one of them attempted to push him around. He could then actually kill a stallion. He must be part Roland.

"THE ARTIFICER"

Buck and Maxwell had been temporarily assigned to Cogburn, the artificer. This was to get all the horses ready for the next engagement.

One afternoon late, they were shoveling out the stables when Captain Miller's aid told Buck he was to report to headquarters.

"What have I done now?" he asked, and hurried to get there.

He was absolutely astounded when he saw his brother, Luke, laconically sipping a cup of coffee and talking with Captain Miller. Luke and Buck ran together hugging and laughing. Luke said, "Pa sent me for Gay Lady and Orso."

Luke was a good looking lad, about seventeen, and everyone kidded him about joining up. He said, "I surly would, but pa told me to get on home as fast as I could and try not to get myself killed.

It was a joyous time with the brothers excitedly telling each other all the news. When they were alone, Buck questioned Luke about the Daniels killing and the sheriff.

Pa said, "Tell you there wasn't no posse sent out, but the sheriff claims there is a warrant for you for escaping jail. Pa said, He didn't think they tried to find you very hard."

Buck asked, "Have you seen Corina?"

Luke replied, "I saw her at the store and she sent you a note."

Buck's hands were shaking as he opened the note and read, "Buck, my life is hell, and I wish you would hurry and get me out of here. I love you forever." There was no signature.

The note helped his feelings, but made him feel desperate and helpless. His regiment needed him and he felt great loyalty to Miller, Maxwell, and the South.

Luke rode off for home astride the family mule and leading

Gay Lady and Orso. It took a big rope to hold Orso because he raised a whale of a ruckus at leaving Buck.

The mule was strong and dragged Orso until he got up and started walking. Buck had tears in his eyes. He sent Corina a note, without signing it, telling her to burn it. He maintained his love for her and promised to come for her. Please wait for me, he begged. He cautioned Luke not to let the note fall into the wrong hands.

At home Corina was being treated coldly and contemptuously by her mother and her brothers. They knew she was sweet on that murderer, Buck Roland. They were not aware that Corina knew who had murdered Joe Daniels.

Buck had become a seasoned mounted infantryman. He was clean, prompt, full of energy, easy to get along with, respectful, and mindful of his duties. He was a good looking Confederate soldier.

When the women camp followers came around the camp, Buck and Maxwell were some of the few that did not bother with them.

Captain Miller and Lieutenant Cogburn, the artificer, were very fond of Buck. They loathed the fact that he might get hurt or maimed by Hondo.

A few days ago, Hondo had broken a trooper's nose. He had made the mistake of cussing Hondo. Hondo spent three days in the regiment's stockade. All this only made him meaner. He spent all of his time in the stockade exercising and lifting weights.

Most of the Cherokees returned to the regiment after the Balsam Mountain raid. One evening they had a huge fire going and were drinking illegal moonshine, chanting and dancing. They sent a runner to bring Buck before the Council.

Buck wondered, "What was this all about?" The Indian,

whose life Buck had saved at high risk to himself, was Black Feather, a Shaman or Medicine Man. Saving him had been, an act of valor that the Indian's could not let go unnoticed. Buck was told where to sit and handed a pipe. He took a long pull, puffed out two huge circles of smoke, belched loudly, and grunted, "Aag, this is good."

All the Council smiled broadly, turned to Black Feather and said, "Now."

Black Feather, with great dignity and ceremony, removed a beautiful fabricated medicine bag from his neck, and placed it over Buck's head. He said, "Wear this and you will live long and well."

Buck realized the great honor bestowed on him and speaking in Cherokee promised to wear it always. He suspected what was in the bag and hoped it did not smell bad.

He was invited to be a Brother and readily accepted. He was now an honorary Cherokee warrior. He was presented with a beautiful stag-horn knife and a handmade axe. In the ensuing conversation he was happy to hear that they knew Flying Wolf. They were aware that Flying Wolf and Buck were good friends.

Miller, who saw everything at the post, soon chose only Buck as the emissary to the Cherokees. Buck was becoming important and trusted by the infantry and the Cherokees. The fly in the ointment was the murder charge hanging over him. Nonetheless, he conscientiously trained for the fight with Hondo which he knew could not be avoided.

Buck and Maxwell sparred constantly. The best help came from the Cherokees. They put their best fighters at Buck's disposal, and brother they knew how to fight. All this was done in secret.

Hondo was completely unaware that Buck could be a problem to him.

A ring had been built behind the horse stable on a hill with a plateau. It was just a square with posts and ropes. A dirt floor was swept smooth. It was hard ground.

Saturday evening before dark was the time set for the fight. The Indians had greased Buck from head to foot. They showed him how to butt with his head, use his teeth, and use both hands and both feet. They even knew about leverage and let him work out with their biggest wrestler.

Maxwell, who was taller and heavier than Buck, worked out with him daily. Buck could handle his fellow scout easily, but old Maxwell was quick and strong. He made a great training partner.

At the time of the fight, Buck weighed one hundred seventy-five pounds. Maxwell had kept up his training sessions with Buck until Buck was in perfect physical condition and his shoulder was well. There was not one ounce of fat on his body.

As part of his training each day, Buck ran three miles through the deer trails around the regiment compound.

His slate colored eyes glistened like diamonds. He was ready for the fight to begin. Buck was fully aware that Hondo would fight dirty, would even try to disable him, and still Buck was not afraid. He believed he could hold his own, and if his medicine worked, he had a chance of winning.

Everyone in the compound turned out for the fight: all the officers, non-commissioned officers, the regular troops, as well as the mounted infantry were there. One noted exception and conspicuous by his absence, was Captain Marcus Miller. The truth be known, Captain Miller thought so much of Buck that it would be like his own son. He thought that the fight would result in a bloody, humiliating, and dehumanizing tragedy for Buck.

Captain Miller had seen Hondo's methods before and they were not pretty. The Cherokees were at the fight, to a man, and in a group by themselves. They were obviously very excited and their favorite was well known. They were a little noisier than usual because they had sneaked a bottle of moonshine on the grounds, and had been sipping it before the fight.

Buck had Maxwell and Black Feather in his corner. They had a little stool, some rags, and a bucket of water.

Maxwell had fashioned Buck a mouthpiece from a big chunk of beeswax. Buck was dressed in his work pants, a BVD shirt, and in his military shoes.

Hondo was stripped to the waist, his work pants held up with a huge leather belt with a rough shaped buckle. He was an awesome sight.

The Sergeant Major announced the way they would fight. He had very few rules. No weapons or foreign objects allowed. It would be a fight to the finish. The Sergeant Major would be the one to call out that it was over and announce the name of the winner.

Buck stood up as Hondo stalked boldly straight to Buck's corner. He slapped at Buck's face with a round house blow with his open hand. Buck neatly stepped aside and moved his head out of the way.

From the force of the blow Hondo stumbled toward Buck. Buck met him with the palm of his hand and up Hondo's nose with all his strength. Blood spewed. Hondo's nose was broken.

By this time Buck was behind him, and kicked his heel tendon knocking his leg from under him. As Hondo was going down, he made a grab for Buck. Buck took his hand, bowed at the waist like a greeting, and went under his arm. Hondo yelled with pain as his arm began to break. He immediately resorted to a dirty trick, kicking Buck in the groin. His feet hit something hard as a brick. The pain in his foot made Hondo think it was broken.

The Indians had fashioned a stiff leather jockey strap, pulled up between Buck's legs and tied to his pants belt in the front and back. This was crude, but very effective. Nowadays they call this a protector, or "the cup."

So far so good! Buck knew he could not hold Hondo's arm, so he let it go and made his way to the center of the ring.

Hondo was bleeding from his nose, and was limping, but remained a dangerous adversary. He weighed two hundred-fifty pounds and stood six feet four inches tall. By normal wrestling or fighting rules this fight would not have been allowed.

Hondo came straight on while Buck waited. Buck recalled what his pa had taught him. With blinding speed, he ran behind the giant and pulled his right leg from under him.

Hondo fell like a tree almost knocking the breath out of him. Buck fell across Hondo's middle and at right angles to him. Buck thought, "Even Hondo cannot move me from this position."

He also had a choke hold on him crushing his windpipe.

Buck thought, "I got him now," only to find himself lifted bodily off the ground and thrown away from Hondo. This man seemed invincible.

For the first time Buck was not confident he could whip Hondo, wondering if he had bit off more than he could chew.

Buck reached up and pulled his mouthpiece out and threw it down. The two men ran together grunting and cursing. Buck levered Hondo over his hip and came down on top of him as hard as he could. He heard Hondo grunt with pain.

Hondo had already closed one of Buck's eyes by using a boxer like punch. Buck knew he had to do something quick. By struggling with all his strength, he was able to get a half nelson on Hondo with one arm, and began beating Hondo on his face and head.

Hondo tried to butt Buck in the face and Buck bit his ear off and spit it in his face. Hondo was tiring rapidly. He had not been in good shape and his breathing was blocked with blood and bone.

Buck relentlessly kept hitting Hondo in the face and on his nose. Finally old Hondo said, "I got enough."

Buck hit him a few more times just in case he was faking it, and then feebly pulled himself off Hondo to a wobbly standing position.

Hondo lay where he was like a dying steer. Buck told Max to bring the bucket of water which he threw in Hondo's face. He then took Hondo by his belt, pulled him upright, and shoved him out of the ring saying, "Shut up, go see the regiment doctor right now."

It was over when the Sergeant Major said, "Buck Roland is the undisputed winner."

It had not been pretty or sportsman like, but Buck had no pangs of conscience. He had accepted this as a fight which would kill or cripple him. For some reason one of his dad's quotes came to his mind, "Son, right is might."

The Indians and Max cleaned their man up and fixed his wounds. They were elated and noisy. Hondo, the legendary regiment bully, had been fairly vanquished.

IT WAS A GOOD DAY.

Hondo was on the sick list for awhile, and refused to speak to Buck

During the noon meal, a few days after subduing the

renegades, Hondo yelled, "You sumbitches, you got all the cornbread." He was angry.

Buck got up handing Hondo his nice warm piece of cornbread, "Take this, I have too much."

Hondo, almost shyly answered, "Is there poison in it Shit Bird?"

Buck kept his cool and said, "No, this is my offer of cornbread and my friendship."

Hondo took the cornbread, turned on his heel without thanking Buck, and ate it with gusto.

The troops prepared wagons and used them to bring the thirty-five dead Confederates back to Waynesville, and buried them in a hastily built cemetery.

Captain Miller quickly readied four hundred prisoners to begin the march of one hundred fifty-eight miles to Salisbury, North Carolina, where they would be jailed in a Confederate Civil War Prison purchased in December of 1861 to house Union soldiers. It was designed for two thousand prisoners, but quickly received ten thousand prisoners. There was plenty of water and shade inside the high walls. However, it soon became over crowded and suffered a shortage of food, medicine, and clothing. The dead were buried in trenches and very likely their identification was buried with them.

On the march to Salisbury, Miller sent some of the Cherokee Indians, one officer, one sergeant, and the artificer, Lieutenant Cogburn. Fifty infantry guards were ordered along. The doctor for Company G accompanied the troops. It would be a forced march, sleeping on the ground, very little fire, and very little care for the sick and wounded.

The Confederate Army, during 1862 in this area, was overwhelmingly outnumbered and poorly equipped. The Southern troops, and especially Company G, had shown in their valiant destruction and submission of the outlaws, deserters, and renegades that they were a formidable fighting force.

Amid much clamor the troops, scouts, the Indians and the prisoners pulled out. To his delight, Buck learned at the last minute, that Maxwell Jones was going with them.

Maxwell was really gung-ho and trying for a promotion, hoping to make Corporal soon. Interestingly enough, Buck was not concerned with awards or promotions. Some of this unconcern was after Captain Miller confidentially confessed to Buck that he had a death premonition. He thought he might be killed after they were engaged at Cumberland Gap. No doubt, the Yankees were a superior force.

With great solemnity Miller said, "I will not dishonor my troops."

Buck knew that he had begun to have doubts of the worth of all of this bloodshed.

Captain Miller had received orders to gather the forces of Company G to join up with the entire 62nd North Carolina Infantry to fight at Cumberland Gap. This was to happen after Company G had deposited the prisoners at Salisbury and returned to Waynesville.

The prisoners were a sorry lot. They behaved because Hondo was told to walk and march with them. He was told to keep them aware of the facts of life. A prisoner will be shot if he causes any consternation which endangers our troops. They took a good look at Hondo and decided it would be best not to take any unnecessary risks.

Buck was returning to the Bivouac from a scouting trip. When he finished caring for Cody, he drank some coffee and got a little breakfast.

Hondo had stolen some rock sugar from the mess supply. He came up to Buck and said, "Here, take this for that dumb and ugly nag of yours." He even cracked a small dent in his stone face with something passing for a semblance of a smile. Buck took it politely and thanked Hondo as he was walking away.

Buck thought better of saying, "Is it poison?"

He wondered if this is a breakthrough with Hondo. Only time would tell.

Captain Miller was doing his job well, but acting depressed. He looked tired and had dark circles under his eyes. His men loved him, and he was taking care of business.

Buck was worried about him and knew that Miller losing his son was terribly hard. Miller was also considering the impending great loss of life of his troops in the upcoming campaign at the Gap.

Captain Miller had heard that his wife was ailing and knew that his daughter was too young for the caretaking responsibilities of his wife's illness. Buck could tell that Miller was close to breaking.

CHAPTER SIX
A Stranger in Buck's Bed

I t was nearly nightfall when the prisoner detail came to a rundown plantation. It must have been one of the largest in the area at one time.

Miller hailed the house from his horse. A striking southern lady came down the path to the gate. She was well dressed although her outfit was worn and thin. Her hair, glossy and brown, was loosely tied in the back and her complexion was fair and unblemished. Her figure was so voluptuous, every eye was upon her. She greeted them politely and Miller advised her he wanted to bed down for the night, feed his troops, and water and feed their horses.

She said, "We have had a few horses before and there is little feed. My father and my eighteen year old daughter are here. My daddy is crippled, and my husband was killed in the battle of Fort Donelson, Tennessee, February 18, 1862. The Yankees have plundered and stole almost everything we had. I can't offer you supper, but after you get your duties tended to, come up to the house for coffee and blueberry cobbler.

As Captain Miller readied himself for his visit to the plantation house, he invited the Field Sergeant, Sergio Verns and Buck to accompany him.

Buck was surprised and honored and set about doing what he could to clean up for the occasion. He washed, put on his one clean shirt, wet his hair down and combed it. He couldn't shave. He did manage to look as good as possible.

The coffee was weak and the cobbler was not sweet, but to the three veterans, it was like caviar. The daughter, Irene, was beautiful like her mother. She had a sad and woeful countenance that was obvious. It was clear she was an emotional wreck. Irene spoke in a very low voice in staccato like sentences.

The old man, Ransom Faulkner, looking every bit the southern plantation owner, was a good conversationalist and had little anger at the war.

In his talk he confided that things had happened to his family that he could hardly bear. "Maybe if the South wins the war we can take up where we left off."

The get together at the plantation ended early on a pleasant note. Laura and her father promised to see them off in the morning.

With no one noticing Irene whispered to Buck, "I need to talk to you."

Buck pretended he did not hear her. Buck asked Mr. Faulkner if he could sleep in the corncrib. It was built off the ground and was dry. The old man agreed.

The three visitors from the army went about seeing to their duties and getting ready to turn in for the night.

Buck took his blankets and fixed himself a nice bed with corn shucks and corn bags. Things quieted down, and everyone being very tired went to sleep early.

Buck was scared speechless when he woke up to find Irene in his blankets snuggling up to him. He almost yelled out in alarm when she whispered, "Please be quiet."

She had her arms around him and her intentions were clear.

Buck only said, "We have to talk."

She then told him, "When the Yankees plundered our

plantation, one of their officers caught me alone in the house and raped me. He paid no attention to my saying, I was a virgin."

When her grandfather found out about this he tried to kill the man, but instead was himself shot in the leg causing him to be crippled.

It was her word against this beast, so the Union authorities took no action against him. The Union troops then left hurriedly.

Irene was very angry and her self worth was nothing. Her grandfather was devastated, but did not want to talk about the tragedy, telling her, "Forget it and tell no one."

Laura, Irene's mother, was a good woman. She was so torn up and emotionally drained, by the rape of her daughter and the death of her husband to be of any help to Irene.

Irene sank into an abyss of silence, anger, and hurt due to her being raped. When she met Buck and looked into his weird, slate colored eyes, and heard his soft, well modulated voice, she knew immediately he could be trusted. She was very surprised to find out she also wanted him.

While telling Buck all this, she tried to stay as close to him as possible. Being a young viral male he had a difficult time remaining objective.

A vision of Corina came before him. He knew he had to help Irene so that she could go on with her life. Buck always remembered what his pa had told him, "Many times an amorous male has no conscience."

Buck had to control himself for Corina and Irene. He held Irene's beautiful, trembling body close, and explained that the easy thing would be to make love to her. "I know we will both feel worthless afterwards."

He went on to explain to her, "You must hold yourself

up and become the young lady you are destined to be prior to the rape. You will meet the right man as if you had been chaste before and since. If he is indeed right for you, he will understand and your relationship will be more secure.

Irene listened carefully and saw the wisdom in Buck's words. She promised she would, and could, follow his advice. She quietly slipped back to her own bed in the house and no one ever knew of their tryst.

Buck thanked his master that he had listened to his conscience and to his heart and mind. He felt good and knew Corina would be proud of him.

The next morning the officers came to the yard fence. The prisoners and guards were lined up behind them for the march. Good-bys and thanks were expressed and to everyone's surprise, Irene opened the gate and walked straight up to Buck. She handed him a cross with a silver chain.

"My grandmother gave this to me; wear it with your medicine bag. I know you will live long and well."

Irene's family was astonished at her gaiety and openness. They were so grateful when Irene became her old self and put her demons behind her.

Buck knew that no one would ever know about this experience except one person named Corina.

Buck looked very handsome when he swung aboard Cody. He was scouting ahead of the marchers and would try to be back for the noon break. It was very rugged country and the wagon trails were not clear. Buck had to be careful of Union scouts and snipers. He kept his rifle handy and made note of everything.

By this time Captain Miller described him as the best scout he had ever had work for him. Buck's lack of ego intrigued everyone. Even old Hondo could not feel enough hate to resist Buck's charisma. Recently, Hondo had dropped by and helped Buck saddle Cody to get ready for his scouting trip.

Buck let him work on their friendship at his own pace. Hondo even told Buck about his past. His hate and hostility stemmed from brutal parents who used Hondo in gambling fights to earn money which they took. He finally ran away and joined the army.

When he met Buck he was bitter, but eventually began to see that Buck's whipping him was a blessing in disguise. He noticed the other men treating him in a more friendly way, and found he liked it.

Buck was blazing the trail for the detail. They had all traversed about eight miles, sitting down to rest, eat hard tack and get one drink of water for troopers and prisoners.

Buck rode by the prisoners as he came into the area. Somehow, cutting his rope tether, a huge Union prisoner came running from the group of prisoners with a sharpened metal rod. His intent was to drive it through Buck's back.

Hondo had been feeding and watering the prisoners. He saw what was happening. Leaping across the heads of the sitting prisoners, and barely in time, kicked the legs from under the big enemy. After that it was only seconds before he had the man helpless.

Buck hastily dismounted, handing Cody's reigns to a passing Confederate guard. Hondo was choking the life out of the prisoner. Buck yelled, "Hondo, let him go."

Reluctantly, Hondo let him up and shoved him toward Buck, saying to the prisoner, "By your attempt to kill Buck, you will suffer a death sentence."

The Union soldier replied, "This man killed my best friend at the spring."

Buck was shaken up, but told Hondo to tie the man back in the line and not to put him on report. Hondo, or the prisoner, could not believe their ears. Buck told them, "One killing does not necessarily create a need for another killing. I am asking that neither of you report this."

The prisoner said, "I honor you for this and I will cause no further trouble."

Hondo told Buck, "You are a fool."

Buck grinned and said, "Not really, I do not suffer fools gladly."

Captain Miller was standing in the shade nearby and had seen and heard it all. Under his breath he said, "Dam, the people's court is good."

He shook his head, walked back to his post, and never spoke of this attempt on Buck's life again in public.

The march was later spoken of as being comprised of the most cooperative Union prisoners ever moved from one place to another.

Captain Miller gave the order to pull out. Cody was well rested and both fed and watered. Miller told Buck, "You and Maxwell ride awhile with me. Your responsibilities as scouts have become more critical and important. Buck and Maxwell were very concerned that their beloved Captain seemed more depressed than ever.

The trip back to the regiment was a hard one but much easier without prisoners, who had been left in the hell hole— Salisbury Prison.

When Buck rode into the regiment ahead of the troops, he reported to the officer left in command. Not much had transpired during their absence.

One more scout had been killed by a Union sniper, who got

away clean. The Confederate scout was a hired, former buffalo hunter, by the name of Wig Jacobson. He was experienced and very dependable.

The Union sniper was using a Whitworth Rifle, British made, which was used primarily by the Confederate Army. It had a hexagonal bore and an effective range of eighteen hundred yards. He could never have gotten close to kill crazy old Wig if he had not had this Whitworth.

Buck was excited to have another note from Corina. It had been handed off at the post by a drummer. The note was brief and unsigned.

"My darling, things are worse than ever here. The sheriff thinks I know who killed pa and keeps asking questions. I need you by my side. Love always."

Poor old Buck almost deserted that night. He resisted the impulse because he knew Captain Miller, Max, and a few more of his buddies might think he was yellow.

It took several days for the prison detail to get back in the routine. Six months to the day after they returned from Salisbury, Captain Miller ordered everyone to fall in before the headquarters office. This was the entire Company G.

Miller was obviously distraught, and told the men that the entire 62nd Regiment, all nine companies including Company G, had been ordered to move out to Greenville, Tennessee.

This was the home of the future President Andrew Johnson. They were to be trained and readied for the fierce fighting at Cumberland Gap.

The morale of Company G was suffering due to being on the move and a shortage of weapons, ammunition, and medical supplies. The cook's were feeding them pretty well because they were getting help from artificer, Cogburn, who brought in wagon loads of harvested vegetables, corn, and any livestock they could confiscate or kill.

Captain Miller's appearance, both mentally and physically, showed his fatigue and worry. Buck found it hard to believe, but it was rumored that Miller was drinking corn whisky he got off the Cherokees.

Buck knew he had to have a talk with the Captain. Despite all these rumors and problems, Captain Miller carried on stoutly. Buck wondered how.

Buck missed his folks and Corina, but was now a soldier, first and foremost. He was in tune with his Captain, his fellow troopers, and with Cody. He was friends with his scouts, and he and Max were best friends.

Orso was on his mind. Did a dog miss his master? He knew Orso liked him and even behaved as if he could read Buck's mind.

In the past when a noise could have cost him his life, Orso was quiet as a mouse. Buck really missed Orso.

One day Buck was in the barn with the stable hands. They dragged Buck over to the feed scales and weighed him like a sack of corn. He weighed one hundred seventy-five pounds. They began laughing and said, "All the caviar, French wine, and cornbread has done made a man out of you."

One of them got a tape measure and backed Buck up against a post. Pull off your shoes cause we want to do this right. In his stocking feet Buck was five feet ten and one half inches tall. This was above the national average which was five feet eight inches and the average weight was one hundred forty three and one half pounds. Buck's build made him look sleek, with long muscles like a panther. His moves were naturally smooth and graceful.

He took all this in good spirits and grinning widely said, "All I want is for Corina to like me."

Buck's voice was low and almost musical. His natural charm came from a great body, strange, but friendly eyes, a ready smile, and a way of making everyone his friend.

His features were regular, with a slightly aquiline nose, a high forehead and a skin that was flawless. He tanned easily without blistering and he always took care of himself. His hair was almost black and glistened in the sun. He had not developed a taste for liquor. Many times he was able to take care of his fellow troopers when they had too much. He had many chips he could call in if needed.

Captain Miller instituted drills and discipline on a daily basis. Something serious was in the wind for the 62nd Company G.

Company G was highly regarded after the capture of the renegades and outlaws, followed by them depositing their prisoners safely at the Salisbury prison.

Buck was very surprised one morning at muster when Captain Miller called him up before the entire company. Buck had slept a little late and did not take time to shave. He said, "I will be reprimanded for my appearance."

He then looked down at his uniform blouse and saw a button was missing. His heart was racing, and he almost went into shock when he saw Max and Hondo by the Captain, holding Cody. "Oh Lord, what have I done?"

To make matters worse Buck saw a paper in Miller's hand. His troubled mind saw this paper as the murder warrant. He marched unsteadily up to Captain Miller, came to attention, and waited anxiously.

In a stentorian voice Miller called up several other troopers to stand in front. He finally turned to Buck and said, "By order of the commander of the regiment Brigadier General J. R. Baxter, you now own Cody. You have been awarded this animal by the Confederate Army in honor and gratitude to your devotion to duty with valor above and beyond thought of your own safety.

You successfully determined the location of the enemy, returned to your company, and led them in a surprise attack. This scouting skill saved many lives."

Buck was overwhelmed when they handed him Cody's reins. Cody was completely saddled and ready to go.

Buck never aspired to accolades, or glory, and therefore was humbly grateful.

"THE INSIDERS"

CHAPTER SEVEN
The Insiders

Captain Marcus Miller was not in the army by conscription. Prior to joining he was a successful Kentucky farmer and plantation owner. His plantation was located in a fertile area where grass, coal, and horses were abundant.

The horses raised in this area, especially the race horses, were fast and very strong. Their bones were extremely healthy because of the natural supplements in the soil.

The plantation was handed down to him by his ancestors. He had one brother who lived and worked the plantation with him on equal shares.

They had a few slaves who came with their inheritance. Brother, Carl, was the hands on overseer and Captain Miller was the business man and politician. They prospered and were happy.

Captain Miller joined immediately after the newly formed Confederate Army, headed up by Southern General Beauregard, fired on Fort Sumter, South Carolina. Captain Miller was firm in his belief in the southern cause.

Due to his readiness to tackle any odds, his obvious administrative and leadership qualities, he was the kind of officer the brigades searched for and promoted as fast as possible. He was also known well enough to be considered a force in the upcoming military campaigns in East Tennessee.

This came about as a result of the intense Union settlement in that area. The victories earned, and strategies employed by Miller resulted in his being promoted to major while he was at Waynesville. This promotion was a very unusual occurrence. There had to be a reason for such an action, and Miller figured he might eventually be placed in charge of the regiment.

His troops were ready, even eager for combat. It was a tribute to the man, that even though his men were poorly armed with not enough ammunition and medical supplies, they remained completely loyal. They continued to hold to their ideals that the south was right, and would ultimately win the war.

Information between the Confederate Armies was inadequate and sometimes non existent. There were exaggerations of victories, and losses, by both sides. Many times surrenders were obtained by one side appearing to be a superior force, while in fact it was the other way around.

At Waynesville, intense training and discipline was carried on. Buck knew that the war was beginning to get vicious and that the outcome was in doubt.

Miller became very careful with whom he talked, and appeared somewhat mysterious. He consulted with Buck daily to learn something new about the surrounding countryside. Buck was riding hard every day. Buck knew that the Union Army was sending its scouts and sympathizers further and further toward Confederate settlements and military encampments. He had some narrow escapes by running into conservatives who favored the Union cause. They would not hesitate to inform on him, or even turn him over to the Union troops.

Facing danger at all times, he was still able to provide

Major Miller the information needed for the safety and welfare of Company G.

Major Miller considered Lieutenant Cogburn, Max Jones, First Assistant Commanding Officer Lieutenant Jethro Thomas, Doctor Aman Summers, and especially Buck Roland as the, "Cinco to Hasta Confiaren", which means in Spanish, "The Five to Trust." A Cherokee Indian once captured by the Mexicans told Major Miller these words.

Major Miller, now gaunt and pale looking, called the five trusted ones to his office. Unlike him, he began by saying, "I will hang anyone of you who betrays my confidence. WE HAVE BEEN ORDERED TO BRIGADE WITH COMPANIES A, B, C, D, E, F, G, K, AND Q AT GREENVILLE, TENNESSEE. We are to quell, kill, and harass any Union forces we encounter. We are to interrupt any supplies intended for the Union, and remember, Greenville is a dangerous place. It is ostensibly a designated training camp. What I have told you is highly confidential. There is no doubt we will have to fight our way to Cumberland Gap, Tennessee. As you may not know, in February, 1862 General Grant issued an order suspending civil government in Tennessee and declared martial law. This came about after the fall of Fort Donelson. Several other bloody battles including Shiloh, Murfreesboro, or Stones River Nashville, and Franklin entered into this design.

Facing his now stern visaged followers, he expounded on his own personal convictions. He glumly and sadly reported that the toll of missing or captured Confederates was grossly understated. "The poor condition of the Confederate Army is far greater than we have been led to believe."

"We have been unable to stop their ships or their troops. We are outnumbered and our supplies are inadequate. I will personally carry on and attempt to be a good officer, and I will never let you down. I ask you to fight with me to the death, if necessary, because I will not surrender."

Rumors were flying in the company. This was due to the scarcity of free travel and information. It became known to the troops, easy enough, that supplies for the South could not be brought in by the river or by railroad.

The Confederates had resistance by way of the Gray Line stretching across the country until that line was broken at Donelson. Laura's husband died at Ft. Donelson where the fighting was the most savage.

It was Saturday night and the Indians were whooping it up. They tried mightily to interest Buck in an Indian squaw and some moon-shine.

Black Feather was especially friendly after Buck saved his life. He was insistent that Buck join with them in their fun and games. Buck was very polite in his refusal of the women and the liquor.

His own fellow soldiers were imbibing also, and somehow persuaded several residents of a brothel to come on the post to bestow their favors. That is, to the few that had a dollar.

Max and Hondo readied themselves to enjoy some female company. Buck tried to talk them out of it. He cited what his pa always told him about getting gonorrhea or something worse.

Hondo laughed and said, "I already had it, it ain't so bad." He went on to say, "I am likely to explode if I don't get some."

Max said he had to get some because he was dreaming about it every night and I just have to get some sleep. Due to the drinking there were a few fist fights of no consequence. The primary problem was the hangovers the next day. As normal,

Major Miller left it up to his subordinates to maintain order. So long as it was taken care of, he busied himself elsewhere.

The men knew better than to try to take advantage of Miller's good nature. He could, and did on occasion, become a veritable tiger. When provoked he was unrelenting.

By this time Miller had grown a creditable set of chin whiskers. On him they looked good. He stayed in close contact with Buck because Buck was his sounding board. It was very striking to observe their relationship. Psychologically, it was plain that Miller observed in Buck all the things he would have desired for his lost son.

Buck, on the other hand, looked upon Major Miller as a mentor or leader to admire and emulate. As the training progressed discipline grew more demanding.

Fatigue resulted in flaring tempers. Mostly there was no flagging of interest "To fight the Union".

After muster one morning, Major Miller ordered Buck to meet him in his office. In a locked back room, the Major stored all the gear from fallen troops, both Confederate and Union.

Miller himself was a great marksman with both rifle and pistol. He ordered the Quarter Master to bring the rifle, shotgun and pistol here. "The weapons I put aside for Buck Roland."

The Quarter Master brought a rifle, shotgun, and a pistol and placed them on a conference table. He saluted the Major saying, "We have completed all the paper work. Is there anything further, Sir?"

After the Quarter Master left, Major Miller explained to Buck that he wanted to be sure that Buck was well armed on his scouting missions. "Our very lives depend on your skills as a scout, and nothing can be left to chance to ensure your safe return. If these weapons please you, check them out and turn in your old weapons to the Quarter Master."

Buck's jaw dropped, and his eyes lit up as he became excited about the awesome weapons. He first picked up the British made Whitworth Rifle. It was used primarily by the Confederate Army and was well known for its accuracy. It was a muzzle loader, forty-nine inches long with a .451 bore and a telescopic sight. It had an effective range of about eighteen hundred yards, and possessed a hexagonal bore which required a hexagonal bullet.

Buck was now drawn to the Sharps sawed off shotgun which was the favorite weapon of the mounted infantry and the cavalry. He said, "What a gun!"

He then reverently picked up the shiny colt a 44 caliber, six shot model. This was a version of the earlier 1848 Dragoon (used in the Mexican Wars). He slid the pistol from its holster and carefully hefted the two pound eleven ounce revolver. He observed that the weapon was in mint condition, but the holster had dark spots on it. Buck knew this was dried blood.

This pistol was taken from a dead Union Captain. Buck's mind was a chaotic mix by this time. One thought kept surfacing like a hungry trout after a fly, "Major Miller was an extraordinary man."

Many mountaineers of the Blue Ridge and Great Smoky Mountains were extremely individualistic. Some of them resented being sent to fight what they considered a non vested interest. They also became fanatically attached to a good leader like Major Miller.

Buck knew he would never let Major Miller down in any way. He did think that Major Miller asked too much of him and many times forgot he was only a scout with short service and little education.

Buck was not especially religious, but his mother declared herself a believer in the midst of her family who she many times described as, "My heathen kin." If necessary she forcibly took them to the little, one-room church several miles from their homestead each Sunday. All of this flooded from the back roads of Buck's mind.

About bedtime Buck walked by Major Miller's quarters on his way to check on Cody. In the stillness of the evening he could clearly hear Miller praying. He was quoting from First John: 5: 13, "I write this to you, who believe in the name of the son of God, that you may know that you have eternal life."

Buck remembered his Sunday school teacher asking them to memorize this passage of scripture. She said with a smile, it is a promise which is better than money in the bank.

While Buck was caring for Cody, he tried to sort out his scrambled mind. He was being moved in different directions by a multitude of circumstances. He knew he had to reduce these factors to their lowest common denominator. His family was foremost in his mind, followed closely by his love and need of Corina, his dog Orso and his horse, Cody. This was followed by his affection and loyalty to Major Miller which included his duty as a soldier. Last, but very important, was the Southern cause and his friends and fellow soldiers.

Buck whispered to Cody, you old son-of-a-gun, many times our responsibility becomes almost intolerably heavy. So far you have learned fast, been obedient, faithful, and untiring. Old Son, I can't make it without you. I thank you for learning the extra things for me. I recall how easily I taught you to kneel down, shake hands, and lie down.

"The last trip when I was lying down behind you the sniper's bullet deflected off the metal part of my saddle horn, saving my life. Buck promised Cody, "Ole Pard, we are together forever or until death do us part."

Cody must have been in tune with the fervor in Buck's voice. He laid his head on Buck's shoulder and nickered very softly.

Tears sprang to Buck's eyes and he whispered, "Thank you Cody.

CHAPTER EIGHT
Four guns, two men, two horses

Major Miller believed Company G was ready to fight. He had only about sixty men now. They were short on everything except raw courage and loyalty to Miller. They were still loyal to the cause of the Confederacy.

It was a chilly morning in the third week of March, 1863 when Miller pulled out with his troops from Greenville. They were heading for Cumberland Gap. Buck had had a birthday, March 13, but they were busy getting ready to leave and no one paid any attention.

At the Gap a Union Brigadier General had taken charge of the Gap. He had 20,000 men under his command. This happened after the Confederates abandoned the Gap in June of 1862.

Major Miller had knowledge that the Confederates had bypassed the Gap with about an equal number of troops. They made it into Kentucky where they successfully severed the Union supply line.

General Morgan, without food, still escaped taking his men safely north through Southern territory. The Confederates then returned and took over the Gap. The South cleared up the shambles the Union Army had left behind. They strengthened the fort, and many skirmishes took place.

The Unionists from Tennessee raided the garrison. 62nd North Carolina Regiment, Company G took part in many small battles as they were making their way toward the Gap through rough, hostile, enemy inhabited areas.

When Company G and its counterpart companies, totaling nine in all, began uniting, they formed a brigade. They would be a far greater force to be reckoned with.

Company G moved in beside Company H which was commanded by Captain Henry Cooper of Jackson County, North Carolina.

Cooper was a renowned pistol sharpshooter and it was rumored that he had fought at least two duels before joining the army (obviously winning them).

The weather turned cold as the rains increased. There was a scarcity of blankets, and many of the men suffered from colds and fever. They lacked food, and all these conditions brought about many health problems and some deaths. Diarrhea was common, and generally these soldiers were very unlike the bunch that had left Greenville.

Buck had been scouting five or six miles ahead of Miller's outfit, and late one evening he was about to ask Cody to swim a small branch of swift water. He quietly led Cody to the edge of the water, and was going down the mud banks, when he saw signs that a large group of Union soldiers had been traveling in the area recently.

The Union Army was ranging far a field to be this far inside Confederate held territory.

Now very alert, he heard a sound like someone crawling. The hair stood up on the back of his neck as he slowly pulled his shotgun from its sheath.

He dropped Cody's reins over a dogwood branch, and although he was unnerved he noticed the beginning blooms as a thing of beauty.

He heard a gasp and felt a hand reaching for his throat.

Turning quickly he shoved the business end of his sawed off twelve gauge into a Union soldiers belly.

As he was about to pull the trigger, he looked into the frightened eyes of a beardless, baby-faced soldier. He immediately thought of a frightened deer.

In his panic the boy had dropped his long rifle. The shotgun was cocked and Buck said, "Boy turn me loose and turn around, or I will have to scatter your ass all over these woods until the creek runs red."

The boy soldier said, "Yes Sir." He backed away and Buck said, "Now put your hands behind your head and tell me why I shouldn't kill hell out of you."

The young soldier was trembling all over, but managed to say, "I ain't done nothin to be kilt for."

"Then why are you here? Are you a sentry or a scout?"

"No Sir, I ain't either of them, I am just lost."

By this time Buck had stopped being afraid and almost laughed aloud. "Where is your horse?"

"I ain't got no horse. I just left our camp and went out to take a crap yesterday and got lost. That's the God's truth. Don't kilt me. I ain't never kilt nobody and I am from Kentucky and I wish I was home."

Buck said, "How old are you boy?"

"I am fifteen years of age now, but told them I was seventeen to git in."

Buck told him, "I can't let you go. You will have to come with me back to my outfit. You can ride behind me on Cody."

The boy asked, "You recon they will kilt me?"

"No, my commanding officer won't kill you, and he will know what to do. You will have to tell us all you know."

He readily agreed saying, "I will, I will, just don't let them kilt me."

Cody did not make a fuss when they rode double. Company G was highly amused to see this baby Union soldier riding behind Buck with his arms around him. Old Cody was still high stepping. You would have thought he was in a parade.

Buck Roland turned his prisoner, named Jessie Helms, over to Major Miller. Jessie told the officer where his outfit was camped, that there were about thirty soldiers there, but they were a food foraging outfit and poorly armed. They had obviously ranged too far from their own command post.

Captain Miller ordered his assistant, Lieutenant Jethro Thomas, to talk to the boy and get a general idea of where they could find the enemy.

Jessie went on to explain they were inexperienced, poorly fed, disgruntled, and disorganized. Miller saw an easy victory.

Buck went out, found the enemy, and returned to his troops without incident. The enemy was camped close to a waterfall which made so much noise it was easy to surprise them. Buck found a very obscure and abandoned two rut wagon trail which went over a half mile high mountain and came down on the other side. By using the wagon trail, Miller could move his army on the back side of the Yankee camp. Cooper could bring his Company H from the other side so that they would be coming at them from both directions.

When the signal went they were supposed to run and ride "Hell bent for leather." If a lightning like assault took place, few casualties would occur and would likely result in a surrender by the Union soldiers.

Buck planned all this out on his way to the command post. He was excited and overcome with the desire to tell Major Miller his plans quickly.

He led Cody a good half mile from the spot where he

believed the skirmish would take place. When he felt safe he rode at a gallop all the way to the camp.

Miller was in his office and Buck turned Cody over to one of the hostlers. Buck asked him to rub him down, feed him only oats, no green stuff, and only give him a small drink of water. "I'll check on him when I get through here. Many thanks."

Buck knocked, saluted, and stood at Miller's door.

Miller raised a weary head and motioned for Buck to sit.

In his excitement Buck called Miller boss. Miller laughed and said, "Sit down Buck, and rest yourself. If you don't calm down you will bust a gut."

"Sir, excuse me, I have got to tell you my idea right away. Can I tell you like I think and no hard feelings?"

"Go ahead son."

"I don't think we should make a frontal attack. We ought to get Company H to hook up with us and find a dim wagon trail that I scouted out. If we will split our troops in half, and come at them from back and side, we will win easily with minimum losses."

Miller looked at this young trooper and thought to himself, "This boy could easily grow up to be a general." He knew in his own heart that he thought too much of Buck, although Buck had earned his trust and affection. They were almost like father and son.

Miller told him to go take care of Cody and report back to him in an hour.

The Major later said, "Company H has agreed to go with us with the plan as outlined. We will pull out at three a.m. and from the intelligence we should be there in about two hours. The Union should still be asleep. Can you and the other scouts take out those sentries?"

"Yes Sir."

Miller and Cooper split up at the wagon trail. Buck and several scouts had ridden out earlier to take care of the Union sentries. For some reason Miller always separated Buck and Max when he could. His explanation was, "You don't put all your eggs in one basket."

Buck personally killed one sentry who chose to fight rather than surrender. Buck cut him deep to prevent noise, but looked away from the man's face as he lowered him to the ground. He could not watch him die.

The next Union sentry was taken care of by a scout using a garrote which he had made from a length of bridle reins.

The third sentry was encountered by Buck because he heard the fight going on. They made their way to the scene to find a Union soldier had butt stroked a Confederate scout on the head, and was standing over him preparing to stab him with his bayonet.

Buck watched as if in a trance as the Confederate scout run him clean through his brisket with his bayonet. They all went to their agreed upon meeting place and waited for Miller, who was advancing as quiet as possible. As planned, they had divided into two groups.

The plan had been good, but its success was hinged on the surprise element. Alas, the Union missed their sentries after which they readied themselves for battle and were coming head-on to Miller's forces. The fighting began. It was a bloody, hand-to-hand, face-to-face meeting of two determined enemy forces.

Miller's troops were superior in size and equipment, but they had lost the element of surprise. This caused a larger loss of Southern troops either wounded or killed. The Union, being fatigued, starved, and sick, lost twice as many soldiers.

Buck was still astride Cody. He had a lot of ammunition left when he saw three Union soldiers talking to what he believed to be the General in charge of the Union forces. The General was sitting on a huge black stallion talking excitedly to two high ranking Union officers. They were behind a large walnut tree.

In the turmoil, Black Feather and this time Max, against Miller's orders, were beside Buck. Buck pointed to the Union General, and pulled his colt shouting, "Let's go."

Cody was tough as whet leather and strong as an ox. He could run like a deer. Buck spurred him which he seldom did. Cody was running at his top speed when Buck guided him full into the black stallion. The colt's barrel was laid neat upside the General's head and he fell from the saddle.

By this time Max and Black Feather had killed the other two. Buck jumped off Cody and told the groggy General he could surrender his troops or die. With Buck's Navy colt at the back of his head the General was given a white flag. He began waving it frantically and shouting, "Cease fire! Cease fire."

The Confederates were getting the better of the skirmish anyway, and the Union soldiers were glad to surrender. It was over.

Miller immediately took charge and arranged for the handling of the Union prisoners. Company G suffered three killed and four injured. Company H had five killed and six injured. The Union had no chance against the combined companies.

After the fighting, Major Miller was talking with Company H Commander, Lieutenant Cooper. Cooper made a snide remark, "I can outshoot any of your scouts." Miller had inadvertently described Company G scouts as sharpshooters, which rankled Cooper. Miller knew Cooper was a crack shot with a rifle or a pistol.

Miller was always looking for clean entertainment for his troops. He turned to Cooper and said, "Let's settle this with a shooting match between you and my scout, Buck Roland."

Buck was not too pleased about being chosen for this kind of duty. Buck said, "I will shoot against him with my pistol and riding my horse."

Word was posted, and Cooper agreed to the terms. A time and place was set. There were ten dried gourds to be hung every twenty-five yards from a swinging tree limb. The rider was to follow the planned route at a full gallop. There would be two events with one score.

The first trip would entail each gourd being shot at with a pistol. After this run the same rider with a twelve gauge sawed off shotgun would shoot at each gourd, still at a gallop. Each rider was going to be timed, and the condition of the gourds examined.

Cooper was riding a red rangy Tennessee stud. He looked very glamorous and confident. Buck was attired in his buckskin clothes and his slouch hat. Cody's coat was washed and brushed until it was gleaming. Cody was acting a little nervous because he did not like the stud. He would have killed him if he could have gotten to him. Buck's shotgun and pistol were cleaned and ready.

Miller fired the starting shot. Cooper was first. He had chosen a .44 Starr pistol. Cooper preferred this weapon because it was a larger caliber.

The stud was well trained and galloped in a straight line. Cooper put a bullet into six of the ten gourds. A slight breeze causing the gourds to move made it a difficult shot. He was disappointed, and voiced his opinion that it was not like shooting a man.

To the next stage, Cooper readied his shotgun, placed his ammo handy, and found that reloading while riding was another tough thing to do. Cooper is good. He shatters eight of the gourds, creditable by any standards.

The men in Company H applauded his efforts, shouting and whooping loudly. It was Buck's time.

Buck found himself a little nervous. He was never of a mind to best another Confederate soldier, but he knew he had to do his best for Company G.

He patted Cody on his bowed neck, pulled his colt and nodded to Major Miller. Major Miller's gun misfired. Buck wheeled Cody around and came back to the starting line.

This time Buck heard the hammer fall and a loud shot. When he turned Cody loose, he was so fast he almost left Buck at the starting point. "Lordy, Lordy, how did I get into this mess," Buck thought.

Cody ran smooth and straight as an arrow. Buck put a shot into six gourds. Company G's applause was thunderous. The Cherokees had turned out in force. Black Feather had started a war dance and shouted, "Stone Eyes," while waving his rifle as a baton. Buck was embarrassed, and told Black Feather to shut up or he would let the Union get him next time.

Buck's comrades were happy, and urged him to do well in the shotgun trial. Another set of gourds were hung.

The breeze had increased as Miller fired the starting shot. Buck tried to use North Carolina wind-age, but all he could do was equal Cooper's record.

"IT WAS A TIE."

Cooper, a real sportsman, rode up to Buck, gracefully dismounted, and said, "Son, I thought I surely could beat you especially riding my Tennessee stud. What is that little horse you have there?"

"Sir, Cody is a thoroughbred Mustang."

This brought a hearty laugh from the troops. Cooper shook Buck's hand and said," You can come and work for Company H."

He pulled a gleaming new jack knife, and handed it to Buck. We gave out no trophies, but I want you to have this to remember our shoot-out. No wonder Cooper's men loved him. There was a close kinship between Cooper and Miller.

Buck's company was ecstatic, and knew what an honor Buck had brought him. They threw him a party that night. They made sassafras tea and somewhere had gotten a hold of some sweet bread.

Gathering around a huge campfire they played a guitar and harmonica. The Cherokees gathered around and sat cross legged, all the while sipping a gourd full of moonshine amongst them.

Max and Hondo got tipsy, and were very pleased when Lieutenant Cooper and his troops showed up and stayed awhile.

Miller and his boys pretended it was Buck's birthday which had taken place a few days earlier.

CUMBERLAND GAP
"The Gibraltar of America"

CHAPTER NINE
What are we Dying For

After the last skirmish Companies H and G were marching steadily on the road to the Gap. Buck and his assistants kept Major Miller and Lieutenant Cooper informed so well that major skirmishes were avoided.

It was still very cold at night. The dogwood was just beginning to bud out. The mountain laurel and wild azaleas were beginning to show a kaleidoscope of vivid colors. There were no vegetables to steal nor were there any berries to pick and eat. The men were lean and mean.

Buck made sure Cody's belly was full and that he never lacked for water. Old Cody was a one man horse, trusting no one except Buck.

All the while Buck kept thinking that this was a no win war, and was convinced it was not worth dying for. All the killing and maiming of human beings had begun to weigh heavily on his mind.

In his scouting trips he had been killing feral hogs for the cooks at the camp. This was beyond his normal duties, but it was not unusual to see Cody bowed up in the back dragging a ninety pound shoat into the camp. "Meat for supper."

Buck was sociable enough, although he was not a follower, and avoided crowds when he could. After he came off a scouting tour, it was not unusual to find him with a blanket, sleeping alone in a wooded area. He was doing his thinking. He was worried because he had not heard from his folks or Corina for a long time. He knew his brother Luke could be somewhere fighting in the war. He was very frustrated that he could not serve the Confederacy and take care of Corina at the same time. "Something has to give," he thought.

Miller was getting more depressed every day. He advised his troops that the Gap was once again in the hands of the Confederacy. Incredibly, the Union, without food, had boldly made their way through Confederate territory to safety.

The work continued on strengthening the seven forts on the North side facing the slope. They cleared the mountain of all trees and underbrush within one mile of each fort.

When Companies G and H arrived at the Gap, they brigaded with several other companies. Lieutenant General Ulysses S. Grant labeled the Cumberland Gap as the "Gibraltar of America".

The regiment had nine companies and about eight hundred men fit for duty. The Confederate Army was scattered all around the Gap. The siege of Cumberland Gap was underway.

The Cherokee Indians, who were good fighters, never faltered and remained with the 62nd, 69th, and other companies all the way.

Buck was losing faith in the cause. The Civil War was marked by staggering casualties on both sides. Some of the military developments, during this time, included rifled muskets, breech loaders, cartridge rounds, repeating rifles, Gatling guns, rifled cannons, ironclad ships, balloons, and submarines.

Over a half million Americans died of wounds or disease, and fifty thousand survivors came home as amputees.

Miller's company was on the South or Tennessee side of the Gap, in Harlan County. On the Harlan County road they were on picket duty. This road overlooked the valley known as Yellow Creek.

Skirmishing and picket firing were continued out on the road. The Union assaulted the regiments with huge numbers, and was trying hard to force the South to leave their positions. No matter how determined the Union was, Miller's men never gave an inch.

Lieutenant Cooper's Company H was stationed on the East Mountain not far away. They were suffering great losses, and appeared unable to hold on much longer.

Major Miller was drinking excessively, managing to carry on bravely although he was not the steady capable leader Buck remembered. Everyone overlooked his drinking, attributing it to the stress of war. It was now May of 1863.

The red buds were ready to come forth, the magnolias and poplar trees were green, and their majestic limbs were waving in the wind.

Buck said to himself, "Yea, I am here sick and homesick as well."

A never before thought of act, leaving the Army, became strong in his mind.

Max Jones had to have his right arm amputated after a wound caused by a sniper's bullet became infected. The surgeon sawed it off near the elbow. All of this came about because of unsanitary conditions and lack of medical supplies.

Buck was a man who always tried to go in a straight line between two points; the shortest way.

He had begun to figure out that no matter who won the war, there were no winners. He had lost a lot of confidence in both Robert E. Lee and Andrew Jackson.

He tried to engage Major Miller in one of their philosophical talks, but Miller was always busy or half drunk.

The last time they talked Miller was bemoaning the number of desertions, the number of wounded, and the lack of supplies. This rendered him unable to fight a good fight. He could not take care of his men. Major Miller was a sick man, caused by frustration, fatigue, and stress. He even hinted to Buck that he might go home.

All this weighed heavily on Buck's mind, and he decided that if things did not change for the better, he would leave. For this possibility, he began caching ammo, horse feed, and non perishable food.

One early morning, as he prepared to ride out to act as a sentry for a number of troops doing manual labor, he noticed that Hondo's horse was not in the stable. He quietly searched for him, but Hondo could not be found. When Hondo failed to show up for muster, Buck knew that he had deserted.

Max was still in the hospital and would be going home soon.

Miller was not capable of bolstering Buck's faltering spirits. He found a poorly scripted note from Hondo which simply said, "Thank you for being my friend, but I am gone." It was signed, "H."

Buck knew in his bones that things were not going good. He always carried the fear of being arrested for a murder he did not commit, but he longed for Corina, and lately was fearful that she would turn to someone else in his absence.

He had no news from his pa and ma, and he continually worried about Luke. Maybe he had not joined up. He wondered if his boyhood Cherokee friend, Running Wolf, could be with the army somewhere. He hoped he would still be in the Cherokee Nation.

It was now June of 1863, and as he was taking care of

Cody, Buck decided to leave the Army and the State of North Carolina. In short, he decided to desert now.

Buck was not a coward, but was convinced he had been carrying on a useless and destructive way of life. He was sure that leaving would be a righteous act, but he told no one.

Miller was now under high ranking officers. Because of his drinking, Company G was only called upon to do picket duty, cut trees and ditches, and any other hard labor task.

Company G was not the glamorous flag waving, rollicking outfit that it used to be, and this demoralized Buck. He was a proud man, and he was going home to Sylva, North Carolina (Western North Carolina). This was dangerous because of the warrant for his arrest, and he knew if he ran into the Daniels it would be a shootout.

He woke early, rolled up his bedding, and went quietly to the stables. He had four guns. The fourth gun he had taken off a Union officer and did not turn in. Buck thought, "I figure I have earned these guns, and Cody is already my horse."

Cody threaded his way through the other horses, and put his head in the halter. He knew something was up. Buck led him by the sentry who whispered, I'll see you tonight. Watch out for them sharp shooters. They are good."

Buck breathed a sigh of relief; so far so good. He had his measly pay in his pocket and his stash of getaway materials. He could not bring himself to think he was deserting. He was not forsaking the army or his friends. In his heart he was not doing this to avoid hazardous duty; his rationale was that he was no longer needed. A real scout did more than patrol for a bunch of laborers. He bade good-bye to Company G about four a.m.

He had begun the arduous and dangerous task of heading south. He began to climb the Smoky Mountains, and was going to try to ride at least ten miles a day.

To avoid capture he was forced to travel by night. He found that due to climbing, he could only make about eight miles during the night; sleeping during the day.

Going down the mountain he would average his nine or ten miles a day. His scouting experience and Cody's color would make it easier.

While he slept he tied Cody's halter rope to his own foot. If Cody were to be frightened and bolted, he could easily kill Buck, dragging him through the trees. This was an unpleasant fact to dream on. He had a hard time sleeping.

The Union was ranging farther and farther abroad and could be expected anywhere in these mountains.

He made very poor time the first night, having to cross a small river which was so deep that Cody had to swim. Buck lashed his guns to the saddle, grabbed Cody by the tail, and pushed him into the water. There was an old saying that a horse who loved water was born a May colt. Cody was a May colt.

He pawed in the water, gleefully making it splash as far as it would spray. Then he would stick his head under water until only his ears showed.

With a mighty jerk his head would come out of the water and he would snort long and loud. Buck prayed he would not do his May colt thing now. No, he slid into the water like a Hippo and swam slowly to the other side. He made little or no noise, and Buck thankfully thought to himself, "Cody, you can read my mind."

He slept and rested on a small plateau about a half a mile high. A giant boulder, surrounded by some walnut trees, gave him a place to hide Cody and get some sleep.

He pulled some soft leaves under his poncho and used his saddle for a pillow. His canteen was full of river water which he hoped was not full of typhoid fever. He had let Cody drink his fill from a small creek, and a hat full of oats completed Cody's dinner.

Unable to build a fire, Buck chewed on a chunk of salt meat and ate a few dried beans which he had soaked in water from his canteen cup. Cody was too tired to run away, so Buck wiped him down and tied his halter rope around a small scrub oak.

Along about midnight Cody began raising cain. Buck thought, "Lord Jesus, I am going to be captured or killed."

He managed to get hold of the halter rope before Cody broke free. He held his muzzle and whispered to him. Holding his shotgun on his lap he waited. He was relieved to find the intruder to be a half grown black bear.

The bear had smelled the meat and was foraging. He was not afraid of Buck, and after shuffling around the dry camp and finding nothing, ambled his way down the mountain.

During this time, Cody was having a fit. A horse is naturally afraid of a bear. Buck had barely enough strength to restrain him.

Another way that he was trying to avoid capture was to smell the smoke from a Yankee's camp fire. They encountered no trouble except the rough terrain and the fatigue of hard climbing.

Buck had often heard it said that the endurance of the Mustang's was incredible. They usually won endurance races. Traveling quiet and steady they made roughly nine miles that night.

They next slept beside a small creek bed. Buck managed to pull enough grass to supplement Cody's dinner of water and a few oats. Buck ate more beans and chewed jerky and salt meat. They rested and slept all day. Their condition was worsening. They were tired, hungry and weak.

Against Cody's wishes, Buck made him lie down. He held up his right front leg and pulled his weight on Cody's neck. While pulling his neck around, Cody had no choice but to go to his knees. He then knew the drill and lay down.

Buck slept close to Cody, and about dusk they set out again. Buck was satisfied with their distance covered in their worsening condition.

This time they found an old log cart road, and were making better progress. They were heading down the mountain which made it easier as well.

Every mile took them further from Union troops, and, with Buck's new found confidence, were traveling both day and night resting only when they could go no further. In the last twenty-four hours they had traveled about fifteen miles. Cody was getting thin and Buck noticed a saddle sore. He walked and led the weakened horse about half the time. He made a poultice, and kept the saddle blanket off the sore with a piece of his shirt. Buck was sorry, but he knew that the hair would come back white after the saddle sore healed.

Another four days of misery and Buck found himself in familiar territory inside the Cherokee Indian Nation. He had already met several Indians, who were either friendly, or hostile. They let him through when he said, "Stone Eyes and Running Wolf."

Buck's spirits were low and Cody was limping a little where he had cut his right front hoof on a sharp rock. The saddle sore was some better, but a long way from being well.

Buck's mind was not too clear due to fatigue, stress and his poor diet. He was very solemn because of the unknown, and was worried about the murder warrant, Corina's condition, and the danger he was bringing down on his own family. He mumbled, "It can't get no worse than this."

Cody continued on although skinny and tired. He never failed a command. His eyes had begun to matter up in the corners even though Buck religiously kept them as clean as he could.

Buck was sleeping soundly when he felt something sticking him in his middle. He came half awake, still in a stupor. The first thing he saw was that the thing in his belly was a rifle barrel.

His eyes followed the barrel up to the owner, and he yelled, "Running Wolf, you scared the hell out of me."

Running Wolf was surrounded by several grinning braves. They had been hunting deer and stealing any horses they could find.

Running Wolf recognized Buck as soon as they slipped up on him. Running Wolf knew Buck was coming. He had received word from the Cherokees at the Gap, and knew Buck had deserted. They fell on each other hugging and laughing out of pure joy.

Running Wolf and some of his tribe had been used sparingly in the near country as hostlers, scout assistants, and hunters. Running Wolf had been elevated to a high rank in his tribe and was looked upon as the next Chief of the Cherokee Indian Nation.

CHAPTER TEN
Family Comes First—Family Reunion

R unning Wolf and his braves finished laughing, and then he and Buck got down to business. His Indian friend agreed to put a message in the hollow tree for Leon. It was a dangerous mission, but Running Wolf smiled and said, "I go where I want to go."

He told Buck they had found a band of horses and made off with them. "We got you a little buckskin mare for Corina," he said smiling.

"I will meet you two days from now, as darkness fills the valley, at Lode Star Springs with the mare. Every Sylva native knew about the springs which were about ten miles away, and emptied into the Tuskasegee River which ran through the middle of Sylva.

The note simply said, "Pa, Ma, Luke, and Nancy, come to Lode Star Springs tomorrow night. Bring Orso. You can get Corina's cousin, Lucy Morgan, to get word to Corina to come with you' all. Don't fail me on any of this for it is my last and only chance," Signed "B."

Running Wolf took Buck and Cody to his village. There was a strange stillness and quiet among the Indians. It was war time, and they were well aware that a white deserter amongst them could only cause them grief; however they would give Running Wolf no trouble. He stilled some of the mutterings by explaining that he and Buck were brothers.

The little Mustang mare was formally presented to Buck. She was about four-years-old with a black mane and tail, and a black stripe down her back. Being the village pet she was fat as a butterball. They were constantly combing her mane and tail and dressing her up in rhododendrons. The young Indian bucks had long since broken her to ride. She was fast as a rabbit, but easily controlled. They had named her Wind Star, after an Indian maiden who was the fastest runner in the entire tribe.

Buck had a gift for Running Wolf. It was a Savage Figure Eight Revolver. It was the .36 caliber revolver. Buck failed to turn it in when he deserted. Buck knew it was worth several ponies and would show to Running Wolf that Buck was a fair and generous friend.

Running Wolf had grown very large for an Indian. He was close to one hundred eighty pounds and was very handsome. He had all the women he could contend with. His chief and all the braves held him in high regard. Different from other high ranking leaders, he talked freely to his men even seeking their advice at times.

Lode Star Springs was a beautiful place, with a well marked wagon trail leading up to a flat cleared area used for camping and picnicking. The spring boil was about fifty feet around, but only six or eight feet deep around the edges of the boil.

A few dare devils swam as deep as they could and claim they never saw the end of it. The spring went underground for ten to fifteen feet before it rushed on out to the coffee colored Tuskasegee River.

The mountaineers living around here were hard working folk, and Buck hoped they would keep working and not come to the springs.

He hid his horse a goodly distance away from the springs.

Three baby coons were up in a small oak tree, and a grown female momma coon became highly agitated at Buck's presence. He made no move toward the babies, and soon the mother called them down from the tree, and they all went scampering off to a safer place, looking back at the interloper occasionally.

When Running Wolf brought the mare to the springs, she was all decorated with flowers by the Indian girls. What a friend. Buck almost asked him to come with him, but knew that Running Wolf would be good for his people, and he did not want to deter him from his leadership of the tribe.

It was almost sunset and Buck was a nervous wreck. The waiting had nearly driven him insane, so much could go wrong. Then he heard a noise. It was a squeaking wheel on a two-horse wagon. He heard the snort of a horse, and the trace chains rattling.

Leon had chosen the two-horse wagon, pretending this was a camping and picnic outing with his family.

Buck lay still, sweat poring from his brow, his eyes squinting trying to see if this was friend or foe. The only noise from the approaching wagon was the wheels turning in the sand, a fart or a grunt at times from the horses, followed by a quiet word or two he could not make out. He could barely control himself, but continued to stay still in order not to make a fatal mistake.

Finally, the wagon came into the clearing and a male voice called, "Whoa Beaner."

Buck breathed, "Lord Jesus," that is pa's voice and their old mule Beaner. Buck made the whippoorwill call and the answering call was surely Leon Roland.

A low growl came from a dog, and he hoped it was Orso. Buck was terribly overwrought with anxiety. What if the authorities had followed his folks? What if one of them was sick or what if Corina did not come?

He couldn't stand it any longer. He stood up very carefully, and called Leon Roland's name very low. Then Leon came forward peering into the dark. As the two forms took shape, they became sure of each other. They approached slowly into each others arms.

Leon had put on a few pounds, and he found his son was taller and leaner, but they now knew that providence had allowed them to meet again. A son who really gets hugged by a real father will tell you it brings on a mystical, ethereal emotion. It is a blend of all good things. If that same father has never let you down, then you will know the feeling.

Leon asked Buck, "Son, are you alright?"

Buck replied, "I have all my arms, legs and teeth, but I have a lot to ask you. Is Ma, Luke, and my sister o.k.?"

"Yes, they are all well, but your Ma has about worried herself to death over you. Did you desert?"

"Yes Sir, I did, and I ain't sorry I did. It was a hard thing to do, but it was the right thing."

Eventually Buck got around to the dreaded question. "Did you get Corina?"

"Yes, she is here."

"What about Orso?"

"Yep, he is here too. We are all here."

Buck asked, "Do you think anyone followed you?"

"No, they are not looking for you, but if they catch you they will obliged to put you in jail. I think they know you did not do it."

Leon shocked Buck when his father said, "I done it. It is the only God-awful thing I ever done in my life. I had to kill him because he was going to kill me and the rest of you. I did not want to bring a killing to my own doorstep. I met him in the woods as I was going to cut wood, and as usual I carried my rifle with me. He was pulling up his overalls when I came upon him."

"He grabbed his rifle and started cussing me and all my kin…said he was gonna kill me and then go to the cabin and kill the rest of you. I couldn't chance my family or you getting killed or hurt. I lifted my rifle and he fired a shot…I could hear it zing by my left ear. I fired from the hip, the bullet catching him in the face. Then I ran. I am sorry I had to do it that way and I will turn myself in if you say so."

"No Pa, I am leaving anyway if Corina will have me. I am taking her with me. I don't know where we will settle, but somehow I will let you know. We are leaving tonight. Don't light any fires, drive this wagon one half mile down the road and wait in a place where we can pull off and unite again. I will be riding a Mustang and leading a Mustang mare for Corina. I will use the whippoorwill call."

Leon hugged him again and said out loud, "Thank you Lord for my boy."

Buck felt better than he had for a long time. In a short while, riding toward the meeting place he saw a figure beside the two-rut road. It was Leon.

Leon whispered, "Buck, come through here."

Two cedar trees were close together with barely enough room to allow them to pass. While he was walking with Leon, Buck heard a sweet voice from heaven. It was Corina crying and trying to talk at the same time. He ran a few steps and gathered her whole body up. Unashamedly she put her legs around his waist and her arms around his neck. They showered each other with kisses. Lordy, Lordy, Buck thought, "Maybe in the dark no one will see this thing sticking out like a pump handle."

He had never before felt like this in his life. Corina kept saying over and over, "I Love You, I Love You."

She looked up above and said, "Thank you Master."

Buck's mother called out, running to her prodigal son. She held Buck close and whispered, "Son, I have missed you so, and I will always love you."

Then it was Luke's and Nancy's turn. Luke was big as a bear and Nancy was looking like a grown woman. All was well at Sylva, North Carolina.

Corina had a small tapestry bag full of her belongings and was ready to leave with Buck. They all had presents for him. Luke had made a stag-horn knife from a straightened out wagon rim. It was sharp as a razor.

Buck undid his belt, sliding the knife and sheath on, and said, "Luke, I won't ever part with this."

They turned to the little mare. Corina asked, "Is it really my horse?"

Buck replied, "Running Wolf presented her to me for you as a wedding gift. She is yours forever."

Goodbyes were made quickly and tearfully. Buck whispered in his pa's ear, "Don't never tell nobody what you told me. I will never tell anybody, on my oath."

"Alright Buck, we will die with this between us."

Leon helped him with directions, telling him to go through South Georgia and stay near the rivers as closely as possible. He could get assistance from the river boats, rafts, and small boats traveling to the Gulf of Mexico. He would also likely find a general store and a grist mill every so often.

Everybody succeeded in hiding their emotions when they parted, except his poor mother. She broke down and clasped Buck to her bosom, and would not let him go. Leon gently took her by the arms and led her away.

Everyone was used to depending on Leon who was always the mainstay of the family. They were all patently aware that it could be years, or never, before they saw these young people again.

The couple took their small amount of necessaries and lashed them behind their saddles. Buck had his ammo and three guns.

With her mountain wisdom, Corina brought with her a few pots, a skillet, and a coffee pot. In a large sack she had smaller sacks of salt, cornmeal, coffee, and dried beans. She knew Buck could shoot the meat. She patted her new horse and smiled graciously.

Her cheeks and eyes glowed with excitement. She was with the man she loved, and was leaving a very distasteful situation at home. She was not treated well by her mother and brothers. The only one she hated to leave was her childhood girl friend, Lucy Morgan.

Orso was beside himself and would make too much noise if allowed to run loose. Buck tied him and Corina's mare to his own saddle. They had enough gear to live on, but not enough to be comfortable. "Who cares," they thought, "We are together."

The first night they spent on the beautiful banks of the Tennessee River in Georgia. They took care of the animals and cooked a rabbit. Orso ate the leavings and seemed to have enough. He weighed almost one hundred fifty pounds, and he worshiped Buck.

Buck, carefully and tenderly, built a bed under some low hanging magnolias. They were tired, but Buck was still horny as a rabbit and Corina was ready.

They grunted and groaned making such sounds of ecstasy they made Orso and Cody restless. Buck apologized for being so quick because of his eagerness. Corina grinned and said, "I hope you want me this bad forever." Later, she asked, "Where are we going?"

"Well baby girl, I have heard that Florida is "The Land of Milk and Honey". We will try to get there, but I warn you we have some hard times ahead."

"Buck, if you teach me, I will stay by your side if it kills me. I ain't no city girl and I ain't fat."

"You sure ain't, you are one pretty thing."

They traveled many miles over land until he found Oconee River in North Georgia. The crossing was dangerous, but they made it without losing a horse or any of their precious gear.

Orso sat on the bank and solemnly watched them splash their way across. They only had to swim a few feet.

While they were slipping and sliding, trying to get up the far muddy bank, they heard Orso yelp as if he was hurt. Then old Orso ran full tilt down the bank and jumped as far as he could in the river. He did not like it, but he was a powerful swimmer, making it across easily.

Corina had gotten wet all over, and when she twisted her skirt it rose up to reveal a cute little undercarriage which Buck viewed proudly, thinking, "All that is mine, whooee."

They continued by land, following cleared areas when they could. Many times they had to travel through palmetto, prickly vines, black jack oaks, and thick underbrush, which caused them to go off their route and proved time consuming.

In spite of the difficulties they finally reached, and crossed, the Oconee River in North Georgia. They paid one of their precious dollars to ride a poorly rigged raft across.

The horses, and Orso, behaved properly, but Buck had a hard time keeping Cody from jumping into the river as they came close to the far bank. Corina asked, "Buck is Cody crazy?"

Buck said, "No, he is a May colt."

Every night Buck fed his animals, took care of the chores, and doused the fire. Then he would make a good bed from whatever soft mat he could find in the area.

For six nights he performed this elaborate procedure, and as soon as Corina was lying down, he would go into lovemaking. They were getting practiced since he serviced her every night. It was kind of funny. On the sixth night as he spread her legs she sighed and said, "Buck, I am taking tomorrow night off. You have just about got me exhausted." They were deeply in love, and all the time he was a tender considerate lover. She responded with equal passion. Buck was a little embarrassed, but lamely agreed.

They continued on land to the Ocmulgee River in Wilcox County, Georgia. They were camped on a sandbar with a tiny fire going at night, when a huge black man spoke from the shadows. "Can I talk to you, Sir?"

Buck cradled the Sharps sawed off shotgun across his body and said, "Show yourself stranger."

When he came into the light, you could see at a glance that he was on hard times. He was a runaway slave named Horatio Jones. Jones had decided to make his way back to his owner's farm in Georgia, saying, "Boss, I ain't found this freedom so good."

He was just hungry and meant no harm. Buck fed him a stewed squirrel and a piece of cornbread. Buck gave him some orders to head out and make several miles from them before he stopped.

Buck told him, "I aim to kill anything that wakes me up." Horatio thanked them and they never saw or heard from him again.

CHAPTER ELEVEN
Way Down Upon the Suwannee River

B uck was constantly amazed how Corina coped with all the hardships they encountered. She not only coped; she brought a joy into their travels by her ingenuity, toughness, and good nature. Buck loved her more every day and as much as she would let him at night.

Cody was a gelding, and surprised Buck when Wind Star came in heat. Cody courted her like a stallion, mounted her, and mated without a problem.

Buck told Corina, "I declare, old Cody is a rig."

"What is that?"

"A rig is a gelding that is not cut clean. He still possesses many of the traits of a stallion. My pa told me all about this one time. I don't think he can get her pregnant, but he can sure help her feelings."

Corina said to herself, "Uh Oh, Buck will come after me tonight."

The saddle sore on Cody's back had healed over. Sure enough, a perfect circle of white hair was coming through. Buck vowed he would never let this happen again.

They met a family traveling north in a one-horse wagon. They were good people who had decided to go back inland, in Florida, and try to settle.

He told Buck about a place called Cooks Hammock, in

Lafayette County, Florida. He explained that it was a rough place, but you can come and go there without questions.

Buck wondered why the man had chosen such a rough place to begin with. Buck liked the part about no questions and did not worry about getting along. He and Corina could get along anywhere.

Before leaving their campsites Buck always made a heap of anything they were leaving and carefully burned it into ashes. He quietly explained, "I don't want no traces of man or woman, nor how many of us there are."

Cody and Wind Star accepted Orso as a partner. A few times Buck and Orso would disappear. Corina would hear one rifle shot and Buck would come back with a medium size feral hog. Good eating. He bragged that Orso was the best hog dog he had ever seen. Orso would lay his chin on his paws until Buck gave him his share of the hog.

With directions from the man in the wagon, they traveled over land until they crossed the Willacoochee River in Coffee County, Georgia, all the while staying close to water. They came to the Alapaha River which was near Jasper, Florida.

At long last they were at the great Suwannee River, the Gateway to Florida. Later the Suwannee River was immortalized by the composer Stephen Foster in the familiar song, "Old Folks at Home." As time went on the entertainer and singer, Al Jolson, made the song "Suwannee" popular. The Suwannee River rises in Southeast Georgia's Okefenokee Swamp and empties into the Gulf of Mexico.

The quintet made their way close to the Suwannee River. They were always thrilled with the beauty of the land near the river. The area was covered with grand moss laden oaks, with arms stretching so high they could easily camp under an oak tree. The sand near the river was snow white although the river ran red from tannic acid.

Buck cut a fishing pole, bought a few hooks from a general store, and commenced to fish. A good fried fish was a welcome addition to their sparse fare.

Corina was brown as a berry and lean as a fox. She was graceful in all her movements. She was elegant as a deer and always smiling and happy.

Buck was learning her so well and he loved to anticipate her wishes. She had never been valued so highly or treated so highly. He had a way about him which let him arouse her easily.

He was exceedingly clean, his hair was usually combed, and he brushed his teeth regularly with salt and an oak toothbrush. The only set back they had was when Corina's foot became infected. It took two or three days to heal. Buck knew what to do. She laughed when he in all seriousness said, "This stuff worked on Cody."

By this time they had spent most of their money. He told Corina he had to work a few days so they could buy some things they needed.

He heard talk of a grist mill on the river near White Springs. He would try there.

A few days later they heard the noise of machinery and came upon the grist mill in operation. The owner, Ebenezer Robinson, a tall slender man warily came out of the mill house. He had his hand in his pocket clutching a small revolver.

He later laughingly told Buck, "Here is what I saw. A beautiful woman on a pretty mare followed closely by a monster dog. Then my unbelieving eyes fell on a figure that would scare hell out of anybody. A big man, with shoulders broad as an ax handle with two guns tied across his saddle. A big Navy colt was on his side. His slouch hat was pulled down and his long black hair and beard fairly glistened."

Ebenezer yelled, "Stop there. What the hell do you' all want?"

Buck in his soft voice, replied, "Just a word with you Sir. I need a job for a few days. I will cause you no trouble."

Ebenezer asked, "What about that beastly sized dog?"

"Sir, that's Orso and he ain't never bit no human yet. He is good at catching hogs though, and he minds me."

"Come on up then."

In a little while Ebenezer was charmed by Corina and Buck and exclaimed with relief, "Yes Sir, I can use you. My wife up and died on me, and I am alone here. She was a good hand at everything, and I miss her terribly."

Ebenezer put Buck to work, and let Corina clean up his cabin.

For miles around folks brought their corn to be ground into crack corn, grits, and meal. It was a thriving business with little or no expense to run it.

Buck shot the meat, and with the corn products they ate well while working for Ebenezer.

Finally one day Buck's earnings had reached ten dollars, and he knew they had to move on. The grist mill business brought too many strangers with too many questions.

Corina reluctantly packed their meager belongings. They saddled up and told Ebenezer goodbye.

Ebenezer had found Orso to be a gentle giant and tried to buy him for twenty dollars. Buck smiled and said, "No Sir, we are together always."

Ebenezer wanted them to stay, "You could settle down here and we could go into business together. We could build you a cabin and be partners."

Buck was honored, but had to go. "Don't tell nobody I been here, and never, never tell my name," he said.

Ebenezer, a true man, replied, "Don't worry son, I will do as you ask."

Ebenezer, a careful man said, "I have to ask you this. Isn't Cody a army horse?"

Buck produced his ownership papers from the army. Ebenezer breathed a sigh of relief. "I just knowed you weren't a thief."

He shook Buck's hand and hugged Corina. She would not have objected to being a grist mill owner's wife if Buck was the mill owner. Buck knew best, however.

They had money and fresh supplies, and they were rested and healthy. They came to a big curve in the Suwannee River and saw a little saw mill with a little village around it. This was Dowling Park, Florida. It contained a store and one or two small buildings.

A landing was noted which led up to a road through the saw mill. They would camp here under the huge, moss laden oaks.

Buck asked Corina to stay at the camp with Orso. He was going to the saw mill to see what was going on. As he approached the saw mill, he saw a few men at work.

He was very surprised when he was confronted by a man as huge as Hondo. The giant was standing in Buck's pathway, and Buck said to himself, "Dam, one of his ears is missing."

The giants first words were, "Sumbitch, what do you want?"

"Nothing Sir, I am camped at the landing and came up here to say howdy."

The giant flexed his muscles and yelled, "I am Sullivan,

and I ain't had my workout today. After I run your ass off, I can go back to work."

He moved menacingly toward Buck. Buck saw in his eyes the lust for a fight. Like quick silver the Navy colt was out of the holster, and aimed at Sullivan's belly button.

Buck whispered, "No I don't have time to fight, only just enough time to kill you."

Any idiot in the world could see what Sullivan saw, a man who would do what he said. Sullivan stood stock still as Buck softly said, "Good day Sir, I hope never to see you again."

Buck was glum as he instructed Corina to get ready and hit the trail. She knew something had happened, but was satisfied to wait until he was ready to tell her. Within thirty minutes they were on their way.

Cody, Wind Star and Orso were tired, but still willing. Buck insisted they travel as quietly as possible. He did not trust that saw mill bunch at Dowling Park.

They moved slowly through the palmettos, grape vines, black jack oaks, cedars, and large oaks. They passed Luraville, on the Suwannee River, without stopping. They noticed a light or two, heard some horses snorting and some cattle lowing. They were entranced by the mystical beauty of the river here and the majestic oaks and cedar trees.

Buck knew from the saw mills and cattle he would probably secure work. He felt in his bones his luck could run out. He could take care of himself, but he feared for Corina's safety.

He had noticed, with distaste, how these isolated, ignorant men from all walks of life were eyeing Corina. She was shapely and beautiful—different than most of the women in the area.

The very traits that made him cherish her so much could

become bothersome. She smiled without guile, and talked to anyone. She was more open than most women.

He met a ferry boat captain when they entered Lafayette County, Florida. They continued traveling near the Suwannee River. The captain, a good man, gave them directions to Cooks Hammock. He confided to Buck, "I have never been there, but I am told it is a very rough place. The law don't even go there. A few federal men have disappeared after going in there looking around with warrants for outlaws, murderers and thieves." Buck decided he would have to go and see for himself. At least they would not turn him in.

He never told Corina what the captain told him, so Corina was happy to hear him say, "We are heading for Cooks Hammock close to where the Suwannee River flows into the Gulf of Mexico."

They were saddle sore, hungry, dirty, scratched, and bug bitten when they suddenly came on a low place where the foliage and trees thickened into a forest.

Campfires were burning down the sides of the one road into Cooks Hammock. A few stick cabins, lean-tos, and temporary structures, which had been hastily slung together, dotted the area. Some of the buildings even had dirt roofs, and a few were covered with palmetto fronds. There was one store and one bar. It was a beautiful, secluded setting. The bar stayed open twenty-four hours a day.

It was nearly nine a.m. when they arrived. They had camped a few miles down the way. Buck pulled Cody to a stop; Orso gave a horrible growl and bared a set of teeth remarkably like a bear.

A man who was obviously three sheets in the wind yelled, "Lord Almighty, a beast from hell."

He ran back into the bar shouting, "You better come see what's out here, a beast from hell and an angel."

Buck told Corina to get Wind Star behind him and keep quiet.

The wing-doors flew open and a massive male stalked out. He had a scatter gun at the ready. Before he said anything Buck recognized him. It was Hondo, who could not believe his eyes and said, "Buck, is that you?"

"Yep, it is. Can we stay here for a few days?"

"Hell yes, you can stay as long as you want. Just remember that Cole Harper is the unofficial law. I work for him, and later I will tell you more."

CHAPTER TWELVE
Cooks Hammock

Hondo was a trusted Lieutenant of Cole Harpers. Cole was a gunfighter who fled to Florida to avoid a murder charge. He had cold bloodedly killed a sheriff in a shoot out in Kentucky.

The inhabitants of Cooks Hammock were runaways, outlaws, deserters, and renegade Indians. They were all fleeing from sordid backgrounds. Fear was the primary tool used to maintain a semblance of order.

There were several gun fights, quite a few fist fights, a few stabbings, and other crimes committed. Theft and disagreements were the norm.

The self-styled leader of this bunch, Cole Harper, was a handsome fast gun who was making money from his store and bar. He welcomed Buck and Corina because Hondo approved of them.

Cole commented that anyone who is a friend of Hondo's could get along with the devil. Hondo asked Buck not to tell about their fight. He said, "My reputation here cannot stand that kind of adverse knowledge."

Hondo led them to a little stick cabin, set off by itself, near a spring. The guy who lived here before shot the farrier and left in the middle of the night. Hondo told them they could have the cabin for seven dollars a month.

Corina looked it over and said, "I will make it work."

Buck commandeered a cow stable and a horse stable for Cody and Wind Star. Orso could stay in the house or in the stable with the horses. This was to be their home.

Corina set to work. She was full of energy, laughing and singing, as she began the task of trying to make this a fit place to live.

Buck was apprehensive when he saw the wicked type of individuals choosing the Hammock as a place to hide. The men were surly, dirty and quick to take offense. He knew he would make no lasting friends here.

Cole saw Buck as a cut above the usual type, and took a liking to him. He did not perceive Buck as a competitor. Buck had his guns hidden, and had stopped wearing his Navy colt. It was hidden in a box under some old blankets. Corina was glad; she didn't want him killed or wounded in a gun battle.

She was bewildered by the women at the Hammock. Cole's woman, Ann Sawyer, treated her very well. She was a curvy blond with a devil may care nature.

Ann was used by Cole to sing and serve at the bar. He had an alcoholic piano player to complete the entertainment.

Buck did not frequent the saloon called "The Pigs Breath." Corina knew to stay out of that den of manure.

Ann took to dropping by their cabin to talk to Corina on occasion. Corina welcomed this diversion. They were developing a friendship.

Buck spent much of his time carefully looking after his animals. Orso was body guard enough for Corina when Buck began to seek work. He rode out on Cody each day looking for a job.

Every instinct made him know this was not a permanent home for them. Cole Harper was instrumental in helping him with a job at the Drew Buckeye Saw Mill.

Buck first began peeling poles, and when a saw operator fell ill, was rapidly upgraded. It meant a little more money. Buck had observed the operator and was able to not only operate the saw, but kept the old engine running as well. He adapted easily.

In a place like Cooks Hammock, Buck's quiet nature caused distrust and even disdain. He was not rough looking and many of them mistook his clean habits, and failure to join in their antics, as timidity. That was one big mistake.

Buck became adept at walking away. However, he would not tolerate anyone messing with Corina, his horses, or Orso. One look at Orso's size and his teeth was usually enough to turn them away. Although not wearing a gun, Buck always kept his razor-sharp sheath knife on his belt.

He had no tough reputation to maintain; a good thing in this hell hole. His mind was always racing. Buck would only stay here long enough to accumulate a small stake. He aspired to a higher calling.

Oddly, Cole Harper actually liked Buck, as much as he would allow himself to like anyone. He was always a gentleman around Corina.

Buck was eating well and the work he was doing was putting muscle on him. At the end of the day, trudging on foot for home, he wished for Cody.

Corina had made the shack into a tidy little home. One of the local guns had made one or two overtures toward her. Old Hondo twisted his ear and whispered in his other ear, "No more of that."

Buck was relieved, but also felt like he had no business dodging such an issue. His temper was getting short.

Corina showed no signs of dissatisfaction and encouraged

him always. As they were having their meal one evening she whispered, "Buck dear, I have a surprise for you."

"Oh boy, you baked me a pie."

Corina placed her hand on her belly and said, "You are soon gonna be a papa."

Jumping up and knocking his chair over, Buck grabbed her and danced all around the dirt packed floor, shouting over and over, "I am going to be a daddy."

He was excited and happy and wanted their child. "Are you sure?" he asked over and over.

"Yes, I missed my monthly two times."

They were so happy and they knew they would be good parents together.

Corina commented, "We got to get close to a school and a church."

Buck readily agreed.

Corina grinned as she heard him telling Orso, Cody and Wind Star the good news. She was very touched when she heard him pray, "Lord, let me do the right thing."

He had earned enough money to feel comfortable to leave. Buck called Hondo aside and instructed him, "Don't tell nobody I am leaving. I will go in the night. Pretend it is a surprise when you find I am gone."

Hondo promised and forced himself to say what he had never said to any man before. "I will miss you Buck. Which away are you going?"

Buck replied, "I am going up the river, that's all I can tell you."

Corina and the animals were ready. Even Orso and the horses sensed their excitement. The happy couple secretly packed and got ready for the road.

At his job he had cultivated the confidence and friendship

of his boss, Hiram Starling, who gave him a note to another Drew Buckeye Saw Mill and Logging Company at a place called Luraville, Florida.

They had noted Luraville on their way down the Suwannee River. He might have to change his name. A name change might be necessary when he decided to settle in one place. What would a good name be?

It came to him in a dream. His ma silhouetted in a door of the Roland cabin, crying while bidding him goodbye. As the dream continued he clearly heard her say, "Don't ever forget that you are Sam Shannon."

He told Hondo, "I am going. When you wake up tomorrow we will be gone."

He laid out his gear for the trip, noting that it was too much to carry. When Hondo awoke the next morning he saw a bonfire in the back of Buck's shack. It was flaring up and dangerously close to the building. It seemed like Buck had meant to burn it down. "Oh Hell!" Hondo decided to let it burn. "Maybe I won't miss them." As tears slid down his ugly face, for once he felt a true human emotion.

Cole Harper viewed their leaving as a normal happening and promptly forgot them.

Corina was told about the dream Buck had had about a possible new name. He was heading for a new life and getting his wife out of harms way. He was also exhausted and worn out with running. He would run no more.

Corina noted that he was wearing the Navy colt and his knife again. In the back roads of his mind Buck knew he would come to own land in Florida or Georgia and become a farmer. He was dreaming of reaching up over his head to pull fresh corn for his family and his animals.

Luraville would be one stop, because it was a bend in the

river in Suwannee County that he loved. At this juncture the river was magnificent and the farm land fertile. The land would be easy to clear. He knew in his heart that the folks settling this kind of country would be honest and God fearing. They would desire law and order, a church, and a school.

This plan had rung the bell of certainty that indeed this would be the end of his running and hiding.

The End

"Nobody ever lives their life all the way up except Bullfighters".
Ernest Hemmingway—"The Sun Also Rises"

EPILOGUE

Before writing Smoky Mountain Roots the Civil War was not foremost in my mind. While writing the book, I came to know Buck Roland and his place in that era, both Civil and Military. As this tale unfolded the more intriguing the community of citizens in his life became, as they shaped, challenged, taught, and puzzled him.

There is more to be learned about Buck Roland as he continues to grow physically, intellectually, and yes, spiritually. Unlike many of his contemporaries, Roland did not succumb to the passion of warfare, but put his actions into a more thoughtful context. There is no question that he is destined to mature in his personality and character; a result of his harrowing experiences as a subject of legal injustice. The Civil War, in which Buck fought—1861-1865 was a caldron agitating the conditions which made the blood letting between the North and the South, between friends and relatives unequalled in the history of this country.

"There is nothing nobler or more admirable than when two people who see eye to eye keep house as man and wife, confounding their enemies and delighting their friends." Homer—Odyssey

ABOUT THE AUTHOR

Ray D. Fortner, Sr.—was born
08/03/1924—Live Oak, Florida.
He attended the following schools:
Anona Grammar School, Indian Rocks,
Pinellas County Florida, 1930-1934
Pine Level Grammar School,
Suwannee County, Florida 1934-1938
Suwannee High School—graduated 1942
Graduated—Bachelors Degree

(continued next page)

University of Florida, Sept., 1949
23 Credit hours on Masters Degree
University of Florida and
Florida State University
Military Service 1943-1946
Schering Pharmaceutical Corp. 1954-1955
Florida State Parole Officer
and Supervisor 1955-1959
23 years Federal Service retired as
Chief U. S. Probation Officer,
Northern District of Florida,
Pensacola, Florida—1982.
U. S. Seasonal Park Ranger—
Stones River National Battlefield,
Murfreesboro, Tennessee—1987
U. S. Seasonal Park Ranger—
Lowell Historical Park, Lowell, Mass.—1989